THE HUMAN SANTAPEDE

Adam Millard was born in Shrewsbury, England, in 1980, and grew up in Wolverhampton. He is the author of the zombie novels, *Dead Cells*, *Dead Frost*, and *Dead Line*, the bizarre novellas, *Zoonami*, *Hamsterdamned!* and *Vinyl Destination*, and the supernatural novels, *Deathdealers* and *The Susceptibles*. He can be contacted through www.adammillard.co.uk.

For
Toby

" Ho-ho-hope you enjoy, mate!"

2014

The Human Santapede

ADAM MILLARD

This Edition Published 2014 by Crowded
Quarantine Publications
The moral right of the author has been asserted

A CIP catalogue record for this book
is available from the British Library

ISBN: 978-0-9928838-9-8

Crowded Quarantine Publications
34 Cheviot Road
Wolverhampton
West Midlands
WV2 2HD

"A good many things go around in the dark besides Santa Claus." – Herbert Hoover

"Everything is theoretically impossible, until it is done." – Robert A. Heinlein

"Elves shouldn't be treated like shit. We're not Mexicans!" – Finklefoot

1

They say, whoever *they* are, that a book should never begin with a description of the weather. It's one of those important rules, like never kicking off with an epilogue or an afterword. However, it was snowing so heavily in The Land of Christmas that they, whoever *they* are, would most likely disregard such a ridiculous rule and instead try to figure out why so much fluffy white stuff was falling from the sky.

It was not unknown for it to snow in The Land of Christmas. In fact, it snowed all year round, except for the odd day where it simply *threatened* to. It was, however, strange for it to piss it down so heavily that you could barely make out the village at the bottom the hill or the brightly-coloured lights stretching from one house to the next. Somewhere beneath that perfect white blanket were a thousand elves, all of them wandering the same thing…

How long can an elf last on a diet of snow-cones and elf-faeces?

"What's it doing out there?" Trixie asked, putting down her book and removing her spectacles. She was ranked in the upper echelon of Elvedom, which meant that she could afford books and spectacles to her heart's content. Sometimes she bought books she didn't even read, and glasses she never wore, but that's what happens when elves become successful. The fact that her husband, Finklefoot, was one of Santa's favourite foremen might have had a little something to do with it.

"Oh, it's bleedin' *lovely*," Finklefoot said, peeling his face from the frozen glass comprising their living-room window. "Nothing but nude beaches and piña-coladas. Hang on…" He held a small hand up, before adding, "I thought I just saw David Hasselhoff running down the street with an inflatable red float."

Trixie shook her head. "No need to be like that," she said. "I was just making polite conversation." She picked up her book – something about fifty grey sheds, though quite why she was reading about drab garden structures, Finklefoot didn't know – and pretended to read it. Finklefoot *knew* she was pretending, for her glasses remained in her lap, and her eyes were about as useful as a chocolate radiator without them.

Great, Finklefoot thought, suddenly feeling very guilty. "I'm sorry, love. I didn't mean to be a dick. I'm just fed up. We've got less than a week to go before Christmas Eve, and we can't even get up to the workshop. If it doesn't knock off soon, we'll be too far behind with the toys to catch up. It'll be another one of *those* years." He was, of course, referring to 1999. Two entire gangs of elves had gone on strike three days before the big one, leaving the workshop nineteen million toys short. Finklefoot and his team had had to improvise, knocking together toys from remaindered bits and thingamabobs. In the end, the Furby went on to be rather successful, but it had been touch and go back there for a moment. The last thing Finklefoot wanted was a repeat.

"It'll stop soon," Trixie said. "Enjoy the break while it lasts. The Fat Bastard hardly pays us enough to lose sleep over a shortfall." In fact, Santa Claus AKA The Fat Bastard, didn't pay them at all. It was an elf's job to make toys, and if you refused to make toys, you were sent to the human world to star in pantomimes and horror films. They had all heard such terrible stories about Wizzle (human translation: Warwick Davis), one of their own, and one of Santa's former favourites. Human children were intentionally frightened at bedtime with tales of giants and witches; the children of The Land of Christmas were told stories of the former elf's fall from grace. But that's what happens when you don't conform. You end up in sitcoms with Ricky Gervais.

"You're right," Finklefoot said as he poured a large glass of eggnog. Personally, he hated the stuff, but it was either that or tap-water, and he knew better than anyone not to touch the stuff. If all the elves in The Land of Christmas were making toys, who the fuck worked at the water treatment plant? No one, that's who, which meant it was probably about as safe to drink as an anthrax and acid cocktail. "I just don't want to have to play catch-up. That's how mistakes happen. One minute you're working on a perfectly ordinary plastic doll, the next you're trying to pull a piece of Lego from its ass. And you know how stressed my gang are at the best of times. Rat only has to see the word 'overtime' and his bowels give way, and the last time Gizzo was under pressure, he almost went around the slinky spindle." The only good thing about that would have been pushing him down the stairs to see if he worked.

"Then tell them to work safely, and at their usual pace." Trixie knew that some of the elves only had two paces: slow and stop. "If we're behind when the big day arrives, then so be it. What's The Fat Bastard going to do? Sack us? I'd like to see him try. If you hadn't noticed, us elves aren't knocking out babies like we used to. He'll have a helluva game trying to replace us."

"He'll import elves in from Poland," Finklefoot said. "They work at twice our speed, and you can fit fifty of them into a house this size without them even complaining."

"Yeah, but will they be as *loyal* as us?"

"*Twice* as loyal," Finklefoot said, "and less likely to steal The Fat Bastard's paperclips."

"Who's been stealing his paperclips?"

"*All* of us." It was, Finklefoot thought, the only way to make the job worthwhile. "So it won't make a blind bit of difference to The Fat Bastard if he has to replace us. He'll save a fortune in office supplies, and we'll be shipped off to the human world to play seven dwarves for the rest of our pitiful lives."

"Don't be so grumpy," Trixie said, pushing the specs onto her tiny face.

"Or Sleepy, or Bashful?" Finklefoot said, pacing nervously from one side of the room to the other. "No, me and the boys are going to have to put in extra shifts to make this right.

Santa's going to work us round the clock. Once this blizzard stops, I don't expect we'll see much of one another." That wasn't such a terrible thing, as far as Finklefoot was concerned. He loved his wife dearly, but there were times when she simply got on his tits. When you're married to a person for three centuries, such things are unavoidable.

"I'll have a word with Jessica. She'll tell him to go easy on us."

Jessica – or Mrs Claus, according to the legend – was an ex-stripper, and had the body to prove it. Many of the elves had the hots for her, and a couple had actually managed to penetrate…her steely exterior. The thing about Mrs Claus was that she had a short person fetish, and when The Fat Bastard wasn't around, she made no effort to hide it. As far as Finklefoot knew, she'd already slept with Shart, Rat, and Gizzo. The only thing keeping Jessica from having a slice of *him* was sitting across the room, her nose pressed into a book about grey sheds.

"In the meantime," Trixie said, "get some rest. You've been standing at that window for three days solid. I wouldn't mind if there was anything to see, but we're snowed in."

Finklefoot tapped at the window, watched as a few particles of snow trickled down the tightly-packed block pressed up against the glass.

"You're right," he said, sighing. "I'm going to bed. Wake me up when it's cleared up." And with that, Finklefoot was gone. Trixie listened to his footfall as it disappeared into the bedroom. Once she was certain he was gone, she put the book down and picked up a large candy-cane (six inches, at least) and a piece of tissue.

She picked the book up once again and smiled. "Just me and you now," she said, reaching down into her knickers, where countless pleasures awaited. If only her husband's sobs weren't audible in the next room. It was awfully off-putting.

2

Santa Claus (AKA The Fat Bastard, AKA Kris Kringle, AKA Father Christmas, AKA He Who Shall Be Obeyed) watched as his wife erotically slid up and down the pole, throwing her long, slender legs in any direction they would go without snapping. She was a sight to behold, a beautiful red-headed minx wearing traditional slutty Mrs Claus garb (you could pick it up from any Land of Christmas sex shop, but this one was handmade, and not particularly well, Santa thought, as it was missing its crotch).

Up she went, down she came, a delicious present that Santa would have normally looked forward to unwrapping, and yet…

This snow was taking the piss.

"What's the matter?" Jessica said, sliding down the pole. "You look preoccupied."

Santa sighed. His thick, white beard did a little dance. "Oh, it's nothing," he said, pushing himself up from his armchair. "I guess I'm just not in the mood tonight."

"It's the *weather*, isn't it?" Jessica slipped a red and white robe around her shoulders and went to her husband's side. God, he was fat. He'd always been a little portly, but the last few centuries, he'd really started to let himself go. "It'll clear up soon. We can always start digging the elves out. Or maybe ship some Polish ones in to finish the job?"

Santa grunted. "That would make sense," he said. "I've heard they don't steal paperclips."

"*See*," Jessica said, rubbing his rotund tummy with a perfectly-manicured hand. "Things are starting to look up already."

Making his way across the room, Santa arrived at the bedroom window, slightly out of breath. "I think it's stopping," he said, staring toward the sky. Was he just being optimistic? Was it ever going to stop? Were his staff okay down there, smothered with snow? He didn't know much about the weather – that wasn't his job – but he knew a thing or two about oxygen, and what happened when it ran out. The last thing he needed was for the snow to clear, only to reveal a whole army of dead, blue elves. Even the Polish contingency would be tough to put to work in a place that had, only recently, generated a thousand deceased Smurfs.

But the snow *was* stopping. For the last three days thick sheets had rained down, and now...now you could make out the stars in the sky.

Jessica stretched a hand around and began to stroke her husband's underbelly. The fact that he even *had* one suggested she ought to start casting her net a little further. *I've always got my elves*, she thought. Small in stature, but not in the trouser department, they satisfied her in ways her husband couldn't. She was particularly fond of Finklefoot's crew. They seemed to know which way their bread was buttered. If only she could convince that foreman of theirs to get in on the action.

"I think everything's going to be okay," Santa said, a smile creeping onto his face (beneath the beard, of course) for the first time that week. "Oh joyous occasion! Oh, how wonderful! Oh, by morning my marvellous toymakers will be free! Free to return to work for no money and very little in the way of choice!"

Jessica Claus didn't think her husband quite grasped the concept of freedom.

"Oh, this *is* good news," Santa said, turning to his wife and pulling her into a tight hug. She could feel the erection through his jingling red trousers.

"Is that what I *think* it is?" Jessica said, smiling, licking her lips sensually.

Santa reached down and pulled free a rolled up scroll. It was his Good Child/Bad Child list. "I must get back to work," he said, rushing across the room as fast as an overweight geriatric could. "Oh, how wonderful! How *remarkable*!" And then he was gone, leaving Mrs Claus standing there, half-naked and feeling generally unfulfilled.

The sooner those elves are free, she thought as a stirring in her loins sent a shudder coursing through her entire body, *the better.*

3

If Santa Claus hadn't been busy celebrating the cessation of the blizzard in his study with a large glass of brandy and a mince pie, and if Mrs Claus hadn't been feeling sorry for herself and yearning for the considerate and amatory touch of an elf –

any elf – they might have noticed the dark, cloaked figure moving through The Land of Christmas below. They might have noticed it, or they might not, for the shrouded individual moved quickly, seemingly impervious to the snow beneath its feet.

The footprints the figure left were quickly, and rather cleverly, expunged by the contraption strapped to its back. Essentially a snow-shovel belted to a pair of whirling, battery-powered standing fans, it did the job for which it was built with aplomb. There was no way the snow could betray him; no way they would ever know who he was, at least not until he was ready for them to.

He looked forward to that moment with an eagerness he hadn't felt for many centuries. It would be like Christmas to him, but then again…wasn't everything?

Slipping between two chimney-tops, which just went to show how deep the snow was, the figure sniggered quietly. Reaching into the large sack draped across his shoulder, he pulled out a large shovel. It was the kind of shovel reserved for burying people, or hitting people devilishly hard across the back of the head, or decapitating mice. It wasn't, therefore, a shovel that had seen much in the way of gardening.

Taking a deep breath and a snort of candy-apple snuff, the cloaked figure began to dig.

And dig.

Dig, dig, dig…

After fifteen minutes of laborious digging, the figure considered forgetting the whole thing and returning to his home, but a voice in his head reminded him why he was doing this, why he *had* to do it, and then he saw it again; the vile and beautiful and disgusting and wonderful and grotesque and gorgeous creation that had come to him just a few nights ago. An image so sickening and delightful that it would have given Satan himself nightmares.

Switching the shovel to the other hand, the figure pressed on. Oh, it was going to be exquisite, and when it was complete, stretching around The Land of Christmas for all to see (at least, all those not *partaking*), he would climb up onto the workshop roof and watch in admiration. Watch as The Fat Bastard led the coiling worm through the streets, hollering out for help, begging for the perpetrator to unstitch him from such a foul and fetid fabrication.

And he would laugh, and so on and so forth, for that was the kind of guy he was.

Dig, dig, dig…

Dig…

Dig…

Clunk!

*

"Jimbo," Sissy whispered into the dark. "Jimbo, was that you?"

Something shifted beside her. "Ugh," Jimbo said.

"Jimbo, did you just make a noise?" She was up on her elbows now, glancing around at the shadows.

"What did it sound like?" Jimbo groggily asked.

Sissy shuddered. "It sounded like *clunk!*. Did you just go *clunk!?*"

Jimbo considered the question, and arrived at a conclusion. "In all my years of making noises in my sleep," he said, "I don't think I've ever gone *clunk!*. I don't think it was me."

There was a moment of silence, and then the sound of snoring.

"Jimbo!" Sissy said, nudging her husband hard in the ribs. "Are you going to go check?"

"Check on *what?*" Jimbo said. "I can't hear anything. Maybe you dreamt it. And could you please not elbow me in the ribs when I'm trying to sleep? It's awfully painful and not at all what one might expect from his beloved."

"If you don't get your ass up right now and check on what's going *clunk!*, I'll cut your little elf cock off and mail it to your mother."

Jimbo swung his legs out of bed. "I'm up. I'm up. Deary me, why's it always got to be about mailing severed body-parts to my mother with you, huh?"

"Just go and find out what went *clunk!*," Sissy said. "I don't want to live in a house that makes strange noises."

Jimbo headed for the door, a door that he could barely discern through the gloom. There was no light coming in through any of the windows thanks to the snow, which meant the house was in a state of perpetual darkness, apart from the twinkling red and green bulbs on the tree, but that was in the living-room. Jimbo had stumped his toe four times before he made it out onto the hallway and collapsed in an untidy pile, clutching at his foot and sucking in air through clenched teeth.

"Was that you?" his wife's voice asked from the bedroom.

"What did it sound like?" Jimbo said, still grimacing.

"*Bump, clobber, shit that hurt, bump, hiss,*" Sissy said.

"Yep, that was me," Jimbo said, clambering painfully to his feet. "Can I come back to bed now?"

"Have you found the source of the *clunk!?*"

Jimbo sighed and shook his head. He was about to tell his wife exactly what he thought of her when he heard it. A *clunk!* followed by a terrible scraping noise. In the other room, Sissy crawled beneath the sheets.

Now that he'd heard it for himself, Jimbo moved across the hallway with extreme caution. In fact, so careful was he, that he was hardly moving at all. The way he saw it, the slower he moved, the longer it would be before whatever had gone *clunk!* ate him.

Unfortunately, the thing that had gone *clunk!* had other ideas. A huge, dark-cloaked figure emerged from the living-room, stepping out onto the hallway like a pro-wrestler climbing into the ring.

Jimbo made a noise he'd never heard before.

"Ahhhhhh," the shadowy hulk hissed as it glowered down at the elf. Then there was a sack, and the intruder was opening it, and Jimbo, frozen stiff with fear, couldn't do anything but watch. "Be a good chap and get in the sack."

Now Jimbo, who was a quarter of the size of the assailant and nowhere near as menacing (elves are many things, but foreboding isn't one of them), figured he had three options. Firstly, he could attempt to talk to the invader; some things could be settled with a nice mug of eggnog and a slice of pud. World War III was rumoured to have been abandoned over a nice cup of tea and a wedge of Battenberg. Option two was to do what the intruder said, but Jimbo wasn't keen on the idea of willingly getting into the sack, since nothing good could possibly come of it. He was hardly going to be whipped off to some sun-kissed island for a fortnight of Mojitos and all-you-can-eat teppanyaki.

Jimbo didn't realise he'd already set option three into effect until he was running for the bedroom.

"There's nowhere to hide," the deep, gruff voice hissed behind him. "Nowhere to run."

"SISSY!" Jimbo said, arriving at the marital bed. "I found the thing that went *clunk!*." Dread washed over him as he realised his wife was no longer cowering beneath the covers. She was gone, *kaput*, as if consumed by the mattress. It was an odd thing for a mattress to do, but this was The Land of Christmas, where anything was possible...

"Don't make this any harder than it has to be," the dark figure said, stepping in through the bedroom door, which was far too small for such a colossal being. And yet it fit anyway, as if its bones contracted and disconnected on one side of the frame and recoupled on the other. It was a rather disturbing thing to watch, like one of those Jihadi beheading videos or a Miley Cyrus concert.

"Please don't kill me," Jimbo said, climbing onto the bed. It was probably not the best move, considering the thing had just devoured his wife. "I'm just an elf, and not even a good one at that."

"Oh, you're not going to *die*," the beastly thing said. "You're going to...*evolve*."

Frowning, Jimbo said, "But evolution takes place over the course of centuries, with minute changes occurring in each generation."

"Yes, awfully tedious process, isn't it?" the figure said. "So, hop in the sack and we can get the show on the road." Jimbo wasn't certain, but he thought he saw a smile beneath its dark hood.

Jimbo sighed and lowered himself down over the edge of the bed. "As long as there's no *death* involved," he said. He skulked across the room, and was about to leap into the intruder's wide-open sack when he saw her above the door, hanging there like some tiny superhero.

Sissy!

The bed hadn't swallowed her after all, which was great news, since beds were so damn expensive to replace.

"*Hi-yah!*" Sissy said, bringing her hand down into a chop as she leapt from the wall. Unfortunately, she hadn't had much practice with home invasions, and the intruder was just so damn *big*. She bounced off his shoulder, rolled down his arm, and landed upside-down in the sack.

Jimbo shrugged and smiled sheepishly. "Don't worry, Sissy," he said. "I'm coming, too." And with that he climbed headfirst into the sack. Two pairs of legs kicked and thrashed as the sack's drawstring sealed them in.

The figure grinned, for he had his first elves. The ghastly creation was underway, or would be once he got this pair back to his lair. He laughed, and laughed, and coughed a little before laughing some more.

4

"This is a public service announcement from The Fat Bast…I mean, Santa Claus. All elves are to report to the workshop this morning. Failure to report will result in loss of job, loss of house, loss of pension, loss of respect, and loss of tenure in The Land of Christmas. The blizzard is over, people. It's time to get back to work."

Finklefoot and Trixie arrived at the workshop early, and yet not as early as some of the others, who were already settling down at their stations with mugs of steaming eggnog. Conveyor-belts were already moving, shifting partially-completed toys from one section to another. On the radio, an elfish version of 'Ding Dong Merrily on High!'

played on loop, and would continue to play until someone decided to change the tape.

It seemed everyone was eager to get back to work, eager to gain back the seventy-two hours they'd lost, eager to put Christmas back on schedule.

"I'll see you in twelve hours," Trixie said, kissing her husband tenderly on the cheek. A couple of his gang watching from across the room began to laugh, but Finklefoot didn't care. They could go fuck themselves.

When he reached his section, Finklefoot began assigning the shift's jobs. "Rat, I want you on heads, arms and legs. Nothing gets past you with appendages missing. If there are any dolls or teddies in the reject bin at the end of this shift, I'll make it my personal goal to convince The Fat Bastard that a career in human Hollywood is all you're cut out for."

"Yes, boss," Rat said, snapping his feet together and saluting Finklefoot.

"Shart," Finklefoot said, turning to an elf that had a face only a mother could love. "You're on batteries. What's the most important rule about batteries?"

Shart grinned. "I'm to remove them from every third box, thus making it a nightmare for some parents on Christmas morning."

Finklefoot nodded. "Gizzo, you'll be on wood construction with me. We've got three million plywood cars and planes to put together this morning, and another eight million this afternoon. You up to the job?"

Gizzo pulled a screwdriver from the pocket on the front of his green dungarees. "I feel the need," he said. "The need for speed." Quite where he'd got such a silly line from, Finklefoot didn't know.

"Right," the foreman said. "That blizzard has royally fucked us over, and it's going to take a miracle to get back on track." Not a miracle, *per se*; just a lot of elbow-grease and as few interruptions as possible.

"Finklefoot!" a voice said. It was a beautiful voice, and one with which he was very familiar. He glanced up to see Mrs Claus leaning sumptuously over the railing above, her long, red hair tucked behind her ears. She'd gone to town on her make-up, and it didn't take a genius to figure out why. The last three days must have been hell for her, what with being marooned with The Fat Bastard and the lack of elf-cock. "Santa would like to have a word with you." And with that she was gone. On the workshop floor, a thousand male elves adjusted their erections to a less painful position.

"Whore," Finklefoot said. "She knows exactly what she's doing."

"I *like* her," Gizzo said. "She does this thing with her mouth, kind of like a suck but a blow at the same time, and it—"

"!" Finklefoot said, cutting the elf off mid-sentence. He marched toward the steel steps at the end of the workshop, ignoring the boisterous chuckles from his gang.

This meeting was going to be a nightmare.

*

"Ah, Finklefoot, my good elf!" Santa said as Finklefoot stepped into his office. "How good to see you. My, how you've changed. Have you put on height?" The Fat Bastard poured himself a large brandy; something about the way he moved across the office, glass in hand, told Finklefoot it wasn't his first of the morning.

Over in the corner, Mrs Claus threw herself around a pole. Finklefoot couldn't help but notice that one of her breasts had fallen out. *On purpose?*

"I'd offer you a drink," Santa said, "but you've got a lot of work to get through today, and the last thing we need is something terrible happening to our most productive elf."

Finklefoot felt something akin to pride wash over him. He was, and had been, the most productive elf for nigh-on two hundred years. In any other profession, that would have been rewarded with a handsome pay-rise, or even a promotion. But being one of Santa's elves was like being an elephant-masturbator – a lot of hard work with very little in the way of benefits.

"What's this about, sir?" Finklefoot said. "I've got a lot of work to be getting on with, and…" He trailed off, suddenly mesmerised by the stripping Mrs Claus in the corner of the room.

"Well," Santa said, sipping at his brandy. "I was just wondering if you and your gang would like to put in a few extra shifts, say twelve of them, you know? Just to get things back on track?"

Finklefoot grimaced. "Twelve extra shifts?" he said. "On top of what we're already doing?"

"That's right," Santa said. "To catch up, so to speak."

"But that would mean working solidly around the clock until Christmas Eve." Finklefoot frowned.

Santa laughed like the jolly fat bastard he was. "Oh yes! You're right!" He took another long slug from his glass. Finklefoot watched as the brandy soaked into his boss's silver beard. "It's either that, or we'll have to ship in some Polish elves, and I know how you all feel about that."

"They're very good at not stealing paperclips," Finklefoot said.

"I've heard that, too," Santa said, with a nod and a smile. "So, what do you say? Care to pull us out the shit just this once?"

Just this *once*? Just this fucking *once*? It wasn't *just this once*. It was every year. Every year something went wrong. Every year, someone fell into the poster-paint vat. Every damn year, some fool accidentally put the voice of Osama Bin Laden in the Tickle-Me-Elmos. Last year, Rudolph had been unable to pull the sleigh after the other reindeers had deemed him worthy of a jolly good buggering. It was always…*something*, and this year was no different.

"We'll do it," Finklefoot said. What choice did he have? If it wasn't his gang working overtime it would be someone else's. At least this way it would be in his hands. He would save Christmas – as he always did – on his own terms.

"Marvellous," Santa said, patting Finklefoot on the top of his head. "I knew I could rely on you to make this right."

Behind her husband's back, Mrs Claus twisted her exposed nipple and licked her lips. Finklefoot crossed his legs and said, "There will be conditions."

Santa, who had been refilling his glass at the Christmas-light-adorned bar, turned and frowned.

"My little fellow, you're hardly in any position to barter. I thought I made myself perfectly clear. Make the toys or star in the next George Lucas blockbuster."

Poor Wizzle, Finklefoot thought. He must have been a little ball of sweat wearing that insidious Ewok suit. "We both know that those rules don't apply to me," he said, hoping that he was right. "I'm what they call in the trade 'indispensable'. Without me, every Christmas would be another Easter. Just a boring thing with cards and chocolate."

Santa's lips curled ever-so-slightly into a sneer. "Go on," he said.

"For the next century, no elf is to be banished to the human world. No more *Star Wars,* no more *Harry Potter,* no more *Snow White and the Seven Dwarves,* and no more body-doubling for Tom Cruise. Elves shouldn't be treated like shit. We're not Mexicans."

Santa scowled. Now, most people are accustomed to the jolly, red-cheeked version of Santa Claus; Christmas cards wouldn't sell quite as well if they featured the expression that he currently wore.

"That's all very well and good," Santa said, his eyebrows knitted together, "but how else will we punish the slackers?"

"You could try *not* punishing them," Finklefoot said. It was a long shot, but worth a try.

"Three lashes with a thorny tree and a force-fed plate of holly," Santa said. "And that's my final offer."

Finklefoot sighed. "Two lashes and a mince pie with bauble-glass in it."

Santa smiled. "You drive a hard bargain, elf. That's why you're my number one."

Then why do I always feel like your number two?
"Then I'd better get to work."

He turned and headed for the door, unsure how the rest of his gang were going to take the news. Just before he reached the door, though, it flew open, and there stood Ahora, the forelady of the jigsaw-puzzle section. She looked horrified, as if she'd only just realised she was an elf after years of believing she was human.

In the corner, Mrs Claus threw a hand over her exposed nipple; as much as she loved elves, she wasn't of that persuasion.

"There will be a very good reason as to why you've barged into my office unannounced," Santa said, crushing a glittery purple ball in his giant hand and allowing the tiny shards to fall through his grasp and sprinkle onto the floor

"Terrible news!" Ahora squeaked. "Sissy and Jimbo haven't turned up for their shift! Oh, this is awful! They were on *cutting* duty. Without them, we're just making cardboard pictures!"

Santa rolled his eyes. "Remind me again," he said. "Which ones are Sissy and Jimbo?"

"*Small* people," Finklefoot said. "Pointy ears. Wear a lot of red and green." He was, of course, being sarcastic, but The Fat Bastard didn't seem to notice.

"Ah, yes. Jimbo and, erm, Sissy. Small, pointy ears...*yes.*" He sipped thoughtfully at his brandy while Ahora skipped nervously from one foot to the other in the doorframe. "I will have to arrange for someone to pay them a visit, make sure they're aware that we're back at full steam today."

Finklefoot edged slowly toward the door.

"Finklefoot!" Santa said, so suddenly that Mrs Claus almost fell off her pole. "Be a good chap and pay a visit to the missing couple before you begin your tremendously tiring shift. Take a thorny tree with you, just in case."

Finklefoot thought about arguing, but it would be futile. Besides, the walk would do him good. Clear his head, so to speak, before embarking on the mother of all shifts. The absent pair had probably just overslept. Yes, that's all it was. Lazy bastards.

Always something, Finklefoot thought as he pushed past Ahora and headed out onto the steel mezzanine. *Always fucking something.*

5

The Land of Christmas was back to normal, inasmuch as you could see the village and the lights and you didn't have to worry about drowning in twelve feet of snow. Trucks beeped through the streets – *Beep! Beep! This vehicle is reversing!* – as pathways were cleared to reveal the cobbled ground. Of course, the trucks were unmanned automatons, since every elf in The Land of Christmas was employed by *Santa Claus Inc.*, and therefore required to make toys up at the workshop. Other than Finklefoot, there wasn't a soul in sight. It was quite unsettling, and as Finklefoot walked through the ominous streets, he found himself checking over both shoulders.

It was silly, really. There hadn't been a crime in The Land of Christmas for many years, and that's if you could call leaving a fiery bag of reindeer poop on someone's porch a crime. Statistics said you were more likely to die in a sleigh crash than be murdered in the village, but again, Finklefoot was wary. If everyone was up at the workshop, who had time to conduct statistical surveys?

31

After almost being squashed flat by one of the automaton snow-clearers (never trust a robotic truck when it indicates left) Finklefoot arrived at the residence of the missing elves. The sign screwed into the front door said 'SISSBO', an amalgamation of their respective names. "Fucking tacky, if you ask me," he muttered, even though no-one had asked him anything.

He knocked three times and waited, huffing a plume of frozen breath at the ostentatious sign. He wondered how his gang were getting on. They hadn't been best pleased with him when he left, as if he should have told The Fat Bastard where to go with his extra shifts. He hoped (yet doubted) they would have calmed down by the time he got back. There was nothing worse than working in an atmosphere; it was extremely counterproductive.

"Jimbo? Sissy?" he called through the door. "Sissbo?" Worth a try. When there was no reply, he reached down and turned the knob, expecting to meet resistance. When the door eased inwards, Finklefoot audibly gasped.

Crime was non-existent in The Land of Christmas, as it has already been established, but that didn't mean elves went around leaving their doors unlocked willy-nilly. People liked their privacy, especially married people, who liked to occasionally engage in acts that single people could only fantasise about. Finklefoot was suddenly very aware that he was standing in the absent couple's hallway.

My god, what if they're copulating? What if I'm here, standing in their house, and they're bumping fuzzies in the bedroom? He wasn't a prude; far from it, in fact. Trixie had once allowed him to pop it in the other hole. But that didn't mean he wanted to barge in on Jimbo if he was taking old one eye to the optometrist.

"Hello?" Yes, it was best to call out. Give them a chance to get dressed, or to finish, or to un-cuff themselves. "It's Finklefoot. I'm in your house. You left your front door open, and now I'm in your house." *That ought to do it*, he thought, and yet when nobody replied, his heart sank.

"Okay," he said, moving slowly along the hallway. "I'm now walking along your hallway with the intention of entering your bedroom. If you are in the middle of fornication, I would very much like you to stop what you are doing and put some clothes on."

Silence.

Well this is just effing wonderful, Finklefoot thought. He reached the bedroom door. He knew it was the bedroom door because all the houses in The Land of Christmas were of the same design. The only way you could tell one from the other was by its décor, and even then it was either glittery green, sparkly red, harvest gold, or white.

He knocked. "Last chance to spit out the butt-plugs." When there was no reply, he turned the knob and pushed.

The door opened up onto an unmade bed, which was odd because elves were sticklers for tidiness. It came with the territory, like the pointy ears, rosy-red cheeks, and propensity to fall down the toilet.

This bed, though, was definitely unmade. It was *so* unmade that Finklefoot had to fight the urge to rush across the room and make it.

"Hello?" he said to the empty room. Elves, though small, would find it extremely difficult to hide in their pantie drawers, which meant that this room was very much empty.

An empty room…

An unmade bed…

A pair of missing elves…

"It's a sign it's Christmas again," Finklefoot muttered, shaking his head in despair.

What was he going to tell The Fat Bastard? Something strange had happened here, something that had prevented two of Ahora's jigsaw squad from making their bed as soon as they'd climbed out of it. And now they were MIA, or MINA (Missing in *Non*-Action) as it were, and Finklefoot had a thousand-and-one things he needed to be doing, things he'd much *rather* be doing than chasing missing elves through the empty streets of The Land of Christmas.

After searching the rest of the house, to no avail, Finklefoot stepped out into the cold, vaporous morning and closed the door behind him. There was a word for how he felt in that moment, but for the life of him he couldn't think of it.

"*Mystified*," he said. Yes, that would have to do.

He began the short trek up the hill, to where Santa sat in his workshop office awaiting further news.

6

"There's a word for how I feel right now," Jimbo said, squirming on the trestle table to which both he and his beloved wife had been strapped.

"Is it mystified?" Sissy asked, trying to pull her arm free of its restraints.

"No," Jimbo said. "It's *fucked*. I feel downright *fucked*."

"This wouldn't have happened if you'd clobbered him in the hallway." There was a certain venom to Sissy's tone that Jimbo didn't appreciate.

"At least I didn't jump in the damn sack," Jimbo said.

"Yes you *did*," Sissy said. "You were in it a few seconds after me."

"I meant, at least I didn't...you know what? I don't want to talk about it."

Sissy glanced around the room. It was cold, very surgical, and not at all... *Christmasy.* There were no lights, no decorations, nothing to suggest they were even in The Land of Christmas any more. The only sound came from a slowly-dripping tap on the other side of the room. At the front of the room, something was covered over with a black sheet.

"What do you think he wants with us?" Sissy asked, unable to bear the silence any longer. "I mean, we're *good* elves. This kind of thing shouldn't happen to good elves. We're not Mexicans."

Jimbo tried to shrug, realised he couldn't, and settled for a sigh instead. "Whatever it is, I don't think we're going to enjoy it. Maybe we should start screaming for help. I mean, we weren't brought far. We must still be in The Land of Christmas. Someone's bound to hear us."

The trouble with that, Sissy thought, was that the *someone* would most likely be the shrouded maniac, and the last thing they wanted to do was piss *that* guy off. "He'll hear us. He'll hear us, and then whatever he was going to do to us, he'll just do worse."

"I think he's going to kill us," Jimbo said, which wasn't the best way to comfort one's wife. "How could he possibly kill us worse than he was already going to?"

Sissy whimpered. "This doesn't happen in The Land of Christmas. This is like something out of a terrible movie; one of those ones with the human kids and the inhuman killers. I don't want to end up roasting on an open fire, Jimbo! I've got too much to give."

Just then, the door sprang open in the only way such doors spring, and in came the shrouded figure. Only now he was wearing a white apron, and blue gloves, and neither Sissy or Jimbo thought he was a qualified baker, which meant...

"Ah, how are my first two subjects on this fine morning?" For a raging lunatic he was awfully chipper.

"You won't get away with this," Sissy said, her head the only part of her off the table. "If you let us go now, we'll forget all about it, won't we, Jimbo?"

Jimbo nodded. "Forget about *what?*" he said, winking at their captor. "Heh."

"That *does* sound like a very good deal," the beast said as he began to unpack a small leather case that neither of the hostages had seen before.

It seemed to contain a lot of sharp things. A lot of things designed to cut and carve and amputate. "However, I brought you here for a reason. On the plus side, you won't be alone for long. Soon you will be reunited with all of your friends. *Better* than reunited. You'll all be as one. Isn't that a lovely thought?"

"Not really," Sissy said. "We can't stand most of 'em."

"It's true," Jimbo added. "If it wasn't for the fact we had to work with them every day, we wouldn't bother. There's nothing more annoying than elves."

Tell me about it, the figure thought. "Unfortunately, you're going to have to get used to the idea." He finished laying out the sharp, cutting things and moved – *danced* – across the room, to where the black sheet hid whatever it was the black sheet hid. "You should consider yourselves very lucky, as you are the first two elves to lay eyes upon my most marvellous creation."

"It's a very lovely sheet," Sissy said. "Black's my third favourite colour, after topaz and mauve."

"Ah," the figure said, reaching up and stroking the corner of the sheet with long, slender fingers. "It is nice, isn't it? I have it in green, too, and I…wait a minute, this isn't about the sheet."

"*I* thought it was about the sheet," Jimbo said. "This is all very confusing."

"I don't think he's the full ticket," Sissy said. "One minute he wants to talk about the sheet, the next he doesn't." To the dark shape with his face buried in his palm, she said, "Have you ever been seen by a professional?"

"Look, can we just all stop talking for a moment? I've got a splitting headache, and I really thought this would go much smoother." The abductor sighed, and after a few seconds, he said "Right. Lady and gentleman, I give you—"

"Is *this* about the sheet?" Jimbo said.

"For fuck's sake," the figure said, yanking the sheet away from the thing it covered. "It's about *this*...not the sheet...nothing to do with the bastard sheet..." He poked and prodded at the crude sketch that had been etched onto the whiteboard. "This, this, this!"

What followed could only be described as an awkward silence. It was the kind of silence that could be heard in doctor's surgeries across the universe, the kind of silence that no-one wanted to break, but someone always, inevitably, did.

"What is it?" Jimbo asked, tilting his head sideways and staring at the rudimentary drawing. He could make out limbs...lots of limbs, and beards...*lots* of beards, and even an antler or two. If it had been drawn by an elf-child, the parent of said child would refuse to put it up on the fridge door.

"I think it's one of those arty-farty cubism thingamabobs," Sissy said. "I liked it better with the sheet on it."

"*This*," the figure said, poking at the drawing so hard that he broke a nail, "is a masterpiece. It is a marvel of modern-day surgery. It is history in the making. It is—"

"A waste of good marker-ink," Jimbo said.

"A waste of good ma...*no*!" The beast was losing his temper. Straightening up, he began pacing back and forth across the room. "He thinks he's so high and mighty up there in his workshop, walking around as if he owns the place. Ho-ho-fucking-ho! Well, not anymore. The time has come for a revolution. The time has come for Santa to suffer. The time has come for—"

"Drawing lessons?" Sissy said.

"I will kill you where you lie," the shrouded figure said. Sissy, sensing he wasn't the type of maniac to throw threats around at random, shut up. "You, my little elf friends, are about to become the first pieces in this meaty jigsaw puzzle." He walked across the room, selected a blade from the vast array laid out on the table, and tested its sharpness with his finger. "Before we begin, are either of you allergic to anything and/or are vegetarian?"

Jimbo shook his head. "I once had a funny turn after eating a piece of calendar chocolate, but don't we all?"

The figure growled. "Then let's make a start. Which one of you wants to be at the front?"

T

"So, what you're saying," Santa said, easing back into his throne and regarding Finklefoot with no small amount of suspicion, "is that you found nothing. That these elves have somehow simply ceased to exist. Is that correct?"

Finklefoot shrugged. He had arrived back at the workshop tired and breathless, and now he was facing the Xmas inquisition. He really wasn't in the mood for it. "They're not at home," he said. "I checked everywhere."

Santa stroked his beard. "Did you check the chimney?" he said. "People get stuck up the chimney all the time." He was, of course, speaking from experience.

"They weren't in the chimney," Finklefoot said. *I hope they weren't in the chimney*, he thought...

41

"Maybe they *killed* each other," Mrs Claus said, sidling up to the great throne and wrapping a long and sensual leg around its arm.

"*Yes,*" Finklefoot said. "And then buried each other in the back yard." His sarcasm went straight over the stripper's head, but Santa's frown suggested he got it just fine.

"This is most troublesome," Santa said, forcing a mince pie between his moustache and his beard. Two chews later, he said, "Has this ever happened before?"

Finklefoot cast his mind back as far as he could. "There was that one time when Rat and Gizzo went missing." He remembered it well, for it caused quite a stir at the time.

"Ah, yes. *Remind* me again; where did you find them?"

"Locked in the liquorice warehouse," Finklefoot said. "Been there all weekend, too, hadn't they?"

"Yes, yes, I remember." Santa huffed, impatiently. "Ate their way through quite a lot, if my memory serves me correctly. Little fuckers."

"Do you want me to check the liquorice warehouse?" Finklefoot said, even though it was the last thing he wanted to do.

"No, I don't think that's necessary," said Santa. "I would have heard from Hattie if she'd opened up this morning only to find a couple of engorged, black-lipped elves running amok."

Hattie Quim was the chief-of-operations over at the liquorice factory, and The Fat Bastard was right. If she'd found Jimbo and Sissy, she would have already been in touch, no doubt with a few stern words and a "keep your feckin' workshop in order!'.

"Well, if there's nothing else," Finklefoot said, backing away from the throne. "I really must be getting on with—"

"We'll go look for them *together*," Santa said, pushing his huge, wobbly form into some sort of neat arrangement, or as neat as was possible with such a cumbersome shape. "Finklefoot and Santa, just like old times."

"We've never done this before," Finklefoot said. "And I really have to get back to—"

"Nonsense!" Santa boomed. His wife clenched her breasts to prevent them from vibrating. "Elves don't just go missing. As your boss and superior—"

Pretty much the same thing, Finklefoot thought but daren't say.

"—I'm ordering you to accompany me on this quest to find Sissbo. We can't have our elves scared of walking the streets at night. This is The Land of Christmas, where joy and laughter are spread like wildfire and chlamydia. We will find those missing elves, and we will parade them in front of the entire workshop before clocking-off time today, or my name's not Kris Kringle, and your name's not Feebleford…"

"Finklefoot, sir."

"*Right.* The first place we're going to check is the stables." Santa took a long, hard slug of brandy and hissed, exhaling his alcohol- and mince-pie-infused breath over Finklefoot. "For all we know, Blitzen's had another titty-fit and rendered them both unconscious."

"Is there anything I can do?" Mrs Claus said, draping herself suggestively over the recently-vacated throne. With her husband gone, she was free to do whatever she so desired, which meant a couple of the boys from the shop-floor would be in for a treat before lunchtime.

"No, my little angel," Santa said, looming over her like some unstable tower made out of jelly and hair. "You just sit there and look sexy until I get back." He kissed her on the nose. "If you need anything, and I mean *anything*, just get one of the elves to do it."

Oh she will, thought Finklefoot. *You can bet your fat ass that she will.*

"I really don't think I'm cut out for this detective malarkey," Finklefoot said, hoping for a last-minute exoneration. "I don't even have a gimmick."

"You're an elf," Santa said. "How much more of a gimmick do you need?"

And so they left the office, and then the workshop, and then the workshop grounds, for the stables were kept a few miles away, where the smell of reindeer shit couldn't hurt anyone's nostrils.

8

"You won't get away with this!" Jimbo said. Well, that's what he'd meant to say, but the way he'd been stitched to his wife's backside prevented it from coming out like that. "*Hmph hmph hmhmhmph ish!*"

"Ooh, that tickles," Sissy said. "And not in a good way. Can you not do that, Jimbo?"

They were both on hands and knees, their ligaments cut to prevent them from standing. Jimbo's face was wedged into his wife's rear; only his wide and frightened eyes were visible above the crack. To be quite frank, both had had better mornings.

The hooded figure wiped his bloody hands on his apron and grinned. The operation had gone better than he'd expected. After all, he was working from a drawing that could have been a Michael J. Fox doodle. Still, he had no need for the sketch. The masterpiece was ingrained in his mind, tattooed on his brain like a…brain tattoo.

"Excellent!" the figure said. "See! I told you it wouldn't hurt, didn't I?"

"You *did*," Sissy said. "But you didn't tell me that you were going to stitch my husband's head to my asshole."

"Surprise!" the figure laughed. "Would you rather it was the other way around? I can always unpick the stitches and start from scratch."

"To hell with that!" Sissy said, tottering on one knee. "We had curry yesterday."

"Then quit whining and get used to your new configuration." He walked across the room, picked up a clipboard, and began to flip pages. The pages were, of course, all blank, but flipping them and staring down at them intently was something that came with the job. You weren't qualified as a surgeon if you couldn't handle a clipboard.

"Why are you doing this?" Sissy whined, forgetting that she'd just been ordered not to.

"It's a long story," the figure said. Actually, it wasn't. Like *'Truths From a Politician's Mouth: An Autobiography'*, it was a very short story, but he couldn't be bothered to go into it. Besides, it was none of her business. If he told her, they'd *all* want to know, and that would ruin the surprise when the time finally came to scream it from the rooftops.

"Is it *Santa*?" she pressed.

"Hmph, humph!" Jimbo interjected.

"No, I will *not* shut up!" Sissy screeched. "If you're going to be hanging out of me like an elfish tapeworm for the rest of my damn life, I want to know why!" To the figure, who looked so smart and…*genuine*, as he flipped through the pages attached to his clipboard, she said, "It's Santa, isn't it? The Fat Bastard's done something to piss you off? Well, join the club, you hooded freak. Nobody likes him, not even his *wife*. Do you see us going around, abducting people in the dead of night, cutting them up and sewing them back together in the wrong order?"

"Hmpherrrr!"

"Will you stop talking, Jimbo. I can feel every breath on my kidney, and I don't appreciate it."

"Both of you pipe down," the maniac said. "Nothing you say will save you. The wheels are already in motion, and things are going to get a lot worse before they get…actually, I was going to say *better*, but they're just going to get worse. Sorry about that."

Sissy did something that she'd been trying to hold in. Behind her, Jimbo gagged.

"Now, I have a little surprise," the lunatic said. "Wait here." He popped out through the door at

47

the end of the room, sticking his head back momentarily to add, "Oh, that's right, you can't go anywhere. Well, stay anyway," before disappearing again.

"*Harumph ergh*," Jimbo said, shaking his head and, subsequently, Sissy's backside.

"Yes, he's definitely a few knives short of a cutlery drawer," said Sissy. "I wonder what he's got against The Fat Bastard. I mean, Santa has a strange way of pissing people off, but this guy…well, this guy's holding quite a grudge."

"*Hmph*," Jimbo opined, rolling his eyes.

"Santa might have slept with the dude's missus?" Sissy repeated. "No, I don't think so. He's punching above his weight as it is with that slut of his. He wouldn't *dare* cheat on her. They're crazy in love."

"*Hermph*!" Jimbo said.

"She's fucking most of the elves at the workshop, including the ugly ones from the guitar-stringing crew?" Sissy didn't – *couldn't* – believe such a ridiculous allegation. Maybe her husband was hallucinating; he had, after all, lost a lot of blood, and inhaled a fair amount of gas. She wouldn't believe a muffled word that passed his lips until they were out of there, separate once again.

Suddenly, something thumped just beyond the door. It was all Sissbo could do to stay on their knees.

"Now, don't give me any shit, you red-nosed cunt," the voice of the maniac hissed. A second later the door flew open, and the hooded beast came in. At the end of his arm was a hand, and in that hand were a set of reins, and at the end of those reins was what looked like a very reluctant reindeer with a nose so bright, The Fat Bastard could have used it to see through fog – if he was so inclined and if the sleigh didn't have headlights.

"Rudolph!" Sissy gasped.

"Rmph," Jimbo concurred.

"Now, he's either going on *your* face," he told Sissy, "or *his* backside." He pointed at Jimbo.

Sissy shook her head. "This must be some kind of nightmare. I'll wake up in a minute, covered in sweat and…you know what? Put the damn reindeer on Jimbo's ass."

"Hmmmmmmmmmmmmmmmmmmmmmmmmm mmph!" Jimbo whined.

What the fuck is going on in here? Rudolph thought, almost certain that the man at the end of the reins didn't know who he was, or how much trouble he was going to be in for kidnapping Santa's most infamous sleigh-puller.

"Very well," the hooded beast said, tugging the recalcitrant reindeer across the room. It was hard work; like shifting a fridge that had been standing in the same place for several centuries. Once the creature's ligaments were cut, though, it would be plain sailing.

This is going terribly well, thought the lunatic. It was shaping up to be the best Christmas ever.

10

The stables were a mess when Finklefoot and The Fat Bastard arrived. Stables are not known for their excessive cleanliness at the best of times, but these were so bad, even the reindeer looked ashamed. There was hay where there shouldn't have been, and the walls had been sprayed with a thick coating of magical deer faeces, though it wasn't so magical when it was dripping down the fixings.

"What's wrong with this picture?" Santa said, glancing around at the moseying reindeer and the mess they'd made.

Finklefoot frowned. "Looks like a stable," he said, "but slightly messier." He couldn't help but feel as if they were wasting their time down here. They should have been in the village, where there was a whole lot more of nothing to be seen.

"What's that *song*?" Santa said. "You know? The one about the reindeer?" He looked perplexed, as if he'd just been given a Rubik's Cube with only three sides.

"Ah, I know the one that you mean," Finklefoot said, nodding. "That annoying one about the bullies."

"That's the one!" Santa said, clicking his fingers. "What does that go like again?"

"Da-da-da-da-da-da," Finklefoot said. It sounded like no song he'd ever heard before, but he was working though the lyrics in his head, and that was what mattered. "Da-da-da-da-da. Dasher and Dancer and Prancer and Vixen…"

Santa grinned. "Da-da-da-da-da…Comet and Cupid and Donner and Blitzen."

They both sang the last part together, though sang was perhaps not the right word for it. "But do you recall…the mast famous reindeer of all! Rudolph the—"

"Where the fuck is *Rudolph*!?" Santa bellowed.

Finklefoot glanced around the stables. They all looked the same to him. It was like trying to pick Happy Feet out of a colony of penguins. But wasn't there something different about Rudolph? Something that made him stand out?

"Is Rudolph the one with the gammy leg?" Finklefoot said.

"No, that was *Olive*. We had her put down three decades ago." Santa moved amongst the reindeer. He looked absolutely mortified. "Rudolph's the one with the bloody great big red nose, and she's not here."

Now Finklefoot was even more confused. "*She*? What kind of name is Rudolph for a lass?"

"No-one knows whether it's a boy or a girl," Santa said, grabbing Vixen by the head and then pushing him/her away again. "We don't have access to Wikipedia up here. I've always thought it a bit of an odd name for a doe. It doesn't make it any easier that both males and females grow antlers. I mean, it's as if God is *intentionally* trying to confuse me."

"Wow, you learn something new every day," Finklefoot said, though he doubted it would prove useful information any time soon.

"She's not here! Rudolph's not fucking here!" Santa was frantic, moving from one reindeer to the next. "A couple of elves going missing, I could probably deal with, but people are going to notice if I'm flying over the cities next week with only eight shagging reindeer."

Finklefoot removed his pointy hat, scratched his head, and said, "Maybe this Rudolph character got tired of being coerced. Is it possible that your most famous reindeer has, for want of a better word, *absconded*?"

Santa gasped. "How *dare* you! My reindeer are extremely happy here." At the opposite side of the stable, Blitzen, Donner, and six other reindeer shook their heads. "No, this is the work of our kidnapper. They've taken Rudolph! Oh, my poor, poor Rudolph!" It was all very melodramatic, like something from a daytime soap-opera. All that was missing was the cheesy background music and fake tears.

It had the desired effect, though, and Finklefoot suddenly felt as if he should say something. "Who *wrote* that song, anyway?"

"What?" The Fat Bastard frowned.

"The *song*," Finklefoot said. "The one about the reindeer. Who wrote it? I mean, shouldn't you guys be getting royalties, or something?"

"Come on," Santa said, marching across the stables with renewed vigour. "We've got a reindeer rustler to find."

Not to mention an elf-abductor, Finklefoot thought. Something very bad was happening, and it was happening a week before the big day, when it would hurt them the most.

Somebody was trying to ruin Christmas…

And for once, it had nothing to do with him.

II

"*Have yourseeeeeelf a meeeeeeerry little Christmas*," the hooded maniac sang as he peeled the flesh away from the elf's buttocks. "Let your arse be light." He laughed. The elf, Jimbo, did not, for he was far too busy shrieking and sobbing and wondering what was going to be left of his derriere once the lunatic had finished with it. He liked his bottom; he'd grown quite attached to it over the centuries. Strange how one doesn't truly realises how important one's anatomy is until it's being flayed from one's personage.

"Oh, *calm* down," Sissy called back across her shoulder. Her husband ceased screaming and rolled his eyes. "Honestly, I've never heard anything *like* it." To their abductor she said, "Don't suppose you have any of that numbing cream, do you? That stuff they use for tattooing wimps? Jimbo's never been very good when it comes to pain. I once had to talk him through a bout of wind. Poor git thought he was dying."

"Unfortunately," the figure said, making an incision just next to Jimbo's crack, "I ran out of numbing cream last week. I had a tricky splinter. Your husband's just going to have to man up and take it like an elf."

"Did you hear that, Jimbo?" Sissy said. "No pain relief. I'd suggest biting your lip but your mouth's a little too far inside me and *OW! You little bastard!*"

In the corner of the room, tethered to a vending machine, of all things, Rudolph whinnied and chuffed. He'd got the gist of what was going on, and he didn't like it one bit. His nose, usually bright and red and at least two-hundred watt, was now dark and soft and about as illuminating as a set of Vauxhall Velox headlights in a mine-shaft.

"Don't worry, Rudy," the dark figure said, dropping a lump of severed flesh into a kidney-shaped bowl. "This is what you've been waiting for. You're the most famous of the reindeer, and for what? For helping Santa out on a foggy night? Not much of a legacy, if you ask me, so I'm going to make you famous for something else, something truly remarkable."

I'd rather you didn't, Rudolph thought.

"You're going to be the only reindeer in The Human Santapede! Won't that be something to tell your grandkids, huh?"

"Wait a minute," Sissy said. "Did you just call it a *human* Santapede?"

Coughing, the maniac said, "Indeed I did."

"But so far you've got a couple of elves and a reindeer, and you plan to put Santa at the front?"

The figure already knew where this was going, but decided to play along anyway. "That's right."

"But we're not *human*. Santa's, technically, not human, and I don't know whether you've noticed, but Rudolph is about as far from human as you can get. It's the antlers, you see. They're a dead giveaway."

The shrouded figure grimaced. He had wondered how long it would be before someone noticed the flaw in his plan. "I'm fully aware that the species involved aren't necessarily human…"

"And yet you decided to stick with the name anyway?" Sissy shook her head and clicked her tongue. Behind her, Jimbo did the same. "Surely The Inhuman Santapede would make more sense."

"Well, I did consider that for a moment," the lunatic said. "But it didn't have quite the same ring to it."

"But it makes more *sense*."

"But it sounds *wrong*!"

"Yes, but people are going to *see* us, aren't they? They're going to see us, and stand back and go 'What's it called?' and another will say 'Oh, it's The Human Santapede,' and then someone will say, 'But it doesn't have any humans in it,' and then another will say, 'Hey, he's bloody right. All I see is elves and reindeer and The Fat Bastard, none of which are human,' and then they'll all just walk away, because no-one likes a cheap display."

"Have you quite finished?"

"Yes," Sissy said. After ten seconds of silence – during which time many cogs and wheels turned and whirred in her head – she added, "You could always put the 'In' part in brackets. I mean, The (In)Human Santapede still doesn't make much sense, but at least it's not—"

"Look, I've already decided," the figure said, untethering Rudolph and dragging the poor beast unceremoniously across the room. "You start putting brackets in things, you're just going to make things worse. That's why Meat Loaf songs are terrible."

"Well, don't say I didn't warn you," Sissy said.

"Hmph, smph!" Jimbo groaned.

"Okay, I'll ask him," Sissy said. "Mr Madman? My husband would like to know if you were going to be removing the reindeer's antlers before you attached it to his arsehole."

"Tell your husband that I *was* considering it, but then his wife mocked my choice of name, and now I'll be leaving the antlers right where they are."

Sissy sighed. "Hubbie, it's time to man up."

Jimbo began to cry.

12

There are certain things that love does to a man, things that turn him to jelly or render him stupid. So when Santa returned to the office to discover his wife dressing and a trio of breathless elves leaving – without making eye contact, of course – he thought nothing of it. Finklefoot, on the other hand, was not in love with Mrs Claus, and therefore knew *exactly* what had just happened.

"Ah, darling!" Mrs Claus said as she rolled her stockings up. "I wasn't expecting you back so soon. I was just instructing a couple of the elves from the RC department on how sensitive the steering controls should be on those new fifteen inch Porsches."

"That's good," Santa said, slumping into his throne. The throne practically called out for help beneath him. "You're doing a fantastic job, Jessica. Keep up the good work."

Mrs Claus smiled; Finklefoot grimaced as he noticed the elf pube protruding from her front teeth. As she limped across the room – elves have notoriously large penises, despite being small everywhere else – she regarded Finklefoot with something akin to disgust, as if she couldn't trust an elf that didn't find her attractive. The fact of the matter was, Finklefoot found her just as attractive as the other elves; he just didn't want sloppy eight-hundred-and-fifty-seconds.

"I take it you didn't find the missing elves," she said, pulling a clear heel onto her left foot.

"Not only that," Santa said, "but some thieving bar steward has taken Rudolph."

"Taken *who?*" Jessica Claus knew less about the reindeer than even her husband. If you were to ask her the difference between a reindeer and a normal deer, she would say the latter came with umbrellas.

"*Rudolph,*" Santa said. "The Red-Nosed Reindeer. You remember all those years ago when we had that bit of fog?"

"Oh, *that* one," Mrs Claus said. "Well, why would they take that one? I mean, is there a black market for glowing noses?"

"Maybe we're missing something," Finklefoot said, edging toward the door. It seemed to be the start of a habit, and if past edgings were anything to go by...

"That's why I want *you* to look into it," Santa said, stroking his beard before wedging a large piece of Christmas pud between it. Lord knows where he'd got it from.

"But I've already told you," Finklefoot said, incredulous. "I'm not a private investigator. I'm just a foreman. A foreman with a shitload of work to do, so if you don't mind..."

"A *promotion*," Santa said, so suddenly that he almost choked on a mouthful of currants. Finklefoot stopped moving and started listening. "How would you like to be my second-in-command? Huh? I've always thought highly of you. We could be like the dynamic duo. Batman and Robin, Starsky and Hutch—"

"Wallace and Grommit," Mrs Claus sneered. To her husband she said, "I thought *I* was your second-in-command." She looked positively humiliated. It was a look, Finklefoot thought, that suited her very well.

Santa grinned sheepishly. "You can *both* be my second-in-command," he said. "As far as I'm concerned, you can never have too many."

"What are the perks?" Finklefoot was genuinely intrigued.

"Well, I'll have to write up a whole new set of perquisites for *you*, since most of my wife's bonuses are of a sexual nature, but I shall make it worth your while, and you'll never have to work overtime again."

"My wife and I would like a bigger house," Finklefoot said. "Away from the rest of the village. Neither of us are anti-neighbour, but we're both a little sick of being woken at five in the morning to the chirpy, high-pitched sounds of '*Hi-Ho, Hi-Ho, It's Off to Work We Go*'."

"I think that can be arranged," said The Fat Bastard.

"Don't let him hold you to ransom," Mrs Claus said, massaging her husband's plentiful shoulders. "One minute they want a bigger house, the next you're calling them Sir and shining their shoes."

"And I want all of my crew, and my wife, to have next year off."

"Sounds do-able," Santa said. "Nobody really likes dolls, anyway. One year without them is hardly going to make a difference."

"And if I find out what's happening here, I want a song."

"What?"

"See," Mrs Claus said. "Now he wants a fucking song."

"It's only *fair*. Rudolph got one for saving Christmas, and that was ages ago. I want a song about how I solved this mystery. I want Elton John to write it, and I want it to be Christmas number one for the next three years running, and played on human radio for the next hundred years or so."

"What if Elton John's busy?" Santa said.

"Then Barry Gibb will do, so long as he doesn't actually *sing* it. I don't want it to be remembered as 'that high-pitched song about that brave elf'."

Santa stood, walked across the room, and poured a large brandy. Though it sounded like three very quick actions, it actually took three minutes, by which time Finklefoot had grown very tired of the intense glower from Mrs Claus.

"Okay. You can have whatever you want." Santa ran a hand over his clammy, bald head. "I just want this solved quickly and discreetly. If news of this gets out to the other elves there will be a national panic. Before you know it, we'll have a whole village of anxious elves, and anxious elves do not a great toymaker...erm, *make*, or something like that."

Finklefoot smiled, unsure if he'd got himself a good deal or not. He hadn't wanted anything to do with this a moment ago, and now he was spearheading it. Now he knew how most American presidents felt.

"Then I'm going to need a way to keep in touch with you," the elf said. There was a very good chance things were about to get dangerous, and if things were about to get dangerous, Finklefoot wanted to be able to notify The Fat Bastard at the drop of a hat.

"Jessica, be a darling and have Scrat bring up one of his walkie-talkie sets," Santa said.

"Anything in particular?" Mrs Claus said to Finklefoot. "You strike me as a *Hello Kitty* fan."

"It doesn't *matter*," said Santa. "Just get one up here, pronto!"

Mrs Claus, visibly offended by her husband's terseness, walked across the room, her hips grinding together like a pair of clubbed seals. She opened the office door and stepped out onto the mezzanine. "SCRAT!" She had the voice of an angel, if said angel had a mouthful of jellied eels. "WALKIE-TALKIES, NOW!" She sauntered back into the office and headed for her pole.

Santa arched his eyebrows. "I might live to regret this, but…" He stood and walked across the office, to where a six-by-eight watercolour of The Fat Bastard himself adorned the wall. He slid the painting slightly to the left, revealing a small safe. "It's not that I don't trust you, or anything, but can you look at my wife for a few seconds while I turn the knobby whatchamacallit?"

"I'd rather not," Finklefoot said, but before he knew it, his eyes had settled upon Mrs Claus as she completed rotation after rotation on the pole. Limbs blurred together to make…well, it looked as if an octopus was having a seizure. Finklefoot had to admit, it was rather mesmerizing. It wasn't until a chubby, heavy hand fell upon his shoulder that he snapped out of it.

"This has been in the Claus family for generations," Santa said. He was holding a small box with gilt trim and red, velvet sides. On the top, engraved into a solid gold plaque, was the name *Claus*. It was, Finklefoot thought, the kind of box that could only contain invaluable treasures. So when Santa opened it to reveal a cheap, plastic water-pistol, Finklefoot checked the corners of the room for hidden cameras.

"It's…it's *plastic*," Finklefoot said. Either Santa was lying about the family heirloom, or he'd completely lost his marbles.

"It's whatever it *wants* to be," Santa said, removing the pistol from its box. "This year, most of the toys we're making are plastic, and so it adapts, to fit in…" He held the water-pistol out for Finklefoot to take. The elf wasn't sure he could trust an object that could alter its material at will. "I want you to take it. It is a very powerful weapon."

"Well, water is often referred to as the bullet of the tap," Finklefoot said, his voice drenched with sarcasm. He accepted the pistol, regardless.

"Ho, ho, ho! It doesn't fire *water*," Santa said.

Finklefoot frowned. "Then what *does* it—"

"You summoned me!" a flustered elf said, practically falling into the office.

"Ah, Scrat!" Santa said. "I trust you've brought a set of your fine walkie-talkies?"

The elf glanced down at the box in his hand. "These are my new Spiderman walkies," he said, with some pride. "They have a good range, and if you push a button on the side, it makes you sound like the Green Goblin."

Santa nodded. "They will do nicely." To Finklefoot, he said, "So what do you say, my dear elf? Are you up to the task of saving Christmas?"

Finklefoot turned the water pistol over in his hand and shrugged. Aren't weapons meant to make one feel safe? Protected? A little better off than *not* having a weapon? "I guess—"

"Fantastic!" Santa said. "Scrat, these things have batteries, don't they?"

The elf frowned. "In the box," he said. "But there's just one, and it's flatter than Britney Spears without auto-tune. Do you want me to get some *good* batteries?"

"That would be useful," Santa said, snatching the box from Scrat and stripping the packaging away with eight stumpy digits and a couple of fat thumbs. It was like watching a muzzled dog attempt to thread a needle.

Finklefoot took a deep breath, and prayed for something to strike him down where he stood.

13

The liquorice factory on the other side of The Land of Christmas was the kind of place that *sounded* nice, and yet had all the endearing qualities of Guantanamo Bay. Elves were crammed so tightly together, there was barely room to swing a dormouse. The conditions could only be described as *iffy*, and the elf in command of the whole thing, Hattie Hermann, was an insidious little creature, with a small, silver bun sitting atop her huge head and a face constructed entirely from wrinkles. She worked the elves hard, and got the respect she deserved (at least to her face), which was why the liquorice factory ran like a tight ship. They were, in fact, three years in front with their stock, and yet Hattie showed no sign of relenting. As far as she was concerned, you give an elf an easy time for one year, the next it's like trying to light a firework that's been left out in the rain. It was best to maintain the merciless schedule, despite the current overstock. Besides, kids loved liquorice. And old people. It was just the fifty year gap between that they needed to work on.

Hattie marched through the factory, dipping her fingers in things that would have scalded a normal elf. Elves leapt to attention, saluting her as she passed. As soon as she was gone, though, fingers were jabbed into the air, and mutterings were made. Occasionally, though very rarely, she would catch one of the workers flipping her the bird, and those were the moments she relished.

Making an example of scallywag elves (or *cunt* elves, as she liked to call them) was what she did best. Sometimes, she would have one dipped in a vat of something boiling; others, she would string up to the ceiling like broken Christmas lights. One of the elves, Ginger Somethingorother, had spent an entire week sitting naked atop the black, liquorice Christmas tree in the foyer. Sitting *atop* was not, perhaps, the best way to describe it, for the branches most certainly went inside the poor fellow. And all because he'd called her a, "Bitch-faced whore from the planet Gofuckyourself." Some people just can't take an insult.

"Taste this!" Hattie said, jabbing a warty finger dripping with goo in the general direction of a terrified worker. The worker-elf gagged, but managed to conceal it with a cleverly-timed cough. "Go on. I'm not moving until you've sucked it off."

The elf, whose name was Blix (not that it truly mattered), slowly moved toward the finger, closing her eyes and trying to control her quivering lips. Hattie grinned, for she was a repulsive little bitch.

"Make sure you get it all," she said. "I hate sticky fingers."

The trembling lips enveloped the knobbly digit, and when they came away the dark goo was entirely gone.

"What does that taste like to you?" Hattie asked, frowning so much that her forehead was almost concertinaed in on itself.

"Finger," Blix said. "And salt."

"That's right," Hattie said, wiping her finger on the worker-elf's apron. "It's too salty. I wouldn't serve that to one of The Fat Bastard's reindeer."

"But I…I followed the recipe to the *word*," Blix said.

"Well that's where you went *wrong*," said Hattie. "Times are changing. Humans don't like salt as much as they used to. They're always campaigning against it. Sugar, too. It makes our job a living hell, but we have to move with the times." She slapped Blix once across the face, hard enough to leave a bright red handprint. "Consider that a warning. Less salt from now on. I'll be back this afternoon, and if I'm not happy, I'll make it my personal goal to have you despatched to the human world, where you will spend the rest of your days playing Munchkin #47 in the West End. Do I make myself clear?"

"Less salt," Blix said, fingering the slap-mark on her cheek. "Got it."

"Good. Now go and wash your mouth out. You don't know where my finger has been." And with that, the worker-elf disappeared in a flurry of arms and legs. Hattie's smile revealed a mouthful of rotten, popcorn teeth; it was one of the downfalls of running a liquorice factory.

She finished her afternoon inspection and headed outside for some fresh air. The automaton road-cleaners had finished clearing the street, which meant that she could once again see The Fat Bastard's workshop up on the top of the hill. Music – *Ding Dong Merrily on High*, of course – drifted across the village. Hattie wished someone would change the tape.

She lit a candy cigarette and exhaled a plume of green and red smoke into the air. Ah, it was like heaven, but without all the righteousness and beards. She'd managed to cut down to fifty-a-day, which was much better than the hundred she'd been smoking, but old habits die hard, and at least she'd knocked the eggnog on the head.

It was snowing again, though not as heavily as the previous three days. Hattie didn't know why The Fat Bastard couldn't simply pick up the whole operation and drop it in the Bahamas. It wasn't as if he'd signed a lease, or anything. There was nothing keeping them there, in the freezing conditions with the persistent snow and occasional fog. *It would be nice*, Hattie thought, *to have a tan, if only for a few days*. She, and every elf in The Land of Christmas, were pastier than a gaggle of Irish sunblock testers.

Hattie finished her smoke, and was about to head back in to the factory when something caught her eye.

A dark shape, just in the periphery of her vision, but when she looked, there was nothing but the corner of the factory and a pile of gathered snow.

Now Hattie wasn't mad, at least not in the psychological sense of the word, and so when she thought she saw something, chances were good that she did, in fact, see something.

"What in the name of buggery...?" She slowly waddled along the cleared path beside the factory wall, being careful not to slip. Someone was there; she could see their breath as it crystalized in the air. Whoever it was, they thought they had the upper hand, but you have to get up early in the morning to catch out old Hattie Hermann. "I'm not in the mood for this," she called out. "Whoever is there, you might as well give up. I've got a splitting headache and a thousand elves to mistreat, so..."

The hulking, dark figure stepped out from its hiding place. "What was it? It was the *breath*, wasn't it? I fucking knew it."

Hattie recognised that voice, but she couldn't quite place her finger on it. The trickster's hood did a remarkable job of concealing his identity.

"Who are you, and what are you doing lurking around my factory like some drunken ninja?"

The shrouded figure hissed. "I'm looking for a few good men," he said. "Well, *elves*, to be more specific, and I have it on good authority that you're a bit of a nasty bitch with elves to spare."

"Now just you hold on a min—"

"I'll make it worth your while," the figure said. "Fifty elves of your choosing and I promise not to include you in my masterpiece. How does that sound?"

"What masterpiece? Who *are* you? Are you a little bit crazy?"

"Miss Hermann, I'm perfectly *sane*," the beast said. "Which is why I'm giving you this opportunity to save yourself."

"I *don't* have elves to spare," she said. "And whoever said I did obviously doesn't know a thing about the liquorice game." She thought in silence for a moment, and the hooded figure watched, licking his jet-black lips with anticipation. "This…masterpiece? Would it have anything to do with the big man?"

"If, by 'the big man', you mean The Fat Bastard, then yes, yes it would."

Hattie's frown turned into something more affable. She looked as if she'd just been told she'd never have to look at another fucking Liquorice Allsort for as long as she should live. "Is it something terrible?" she said, evilly. "Is it something that will annoy him greatly?"

The figure waved her questions away with an indifferent hand. "It's much worse than that," he said, rubbing his spiderlike fingers together. "It's something that he has had coming to him for a very, very long time."

Hattie Hermann turned and marched away, leaving the shrouded maniac standing there, confused and unsure if he should have just knocked her head off when he'd had a chance. Then she stopped and turned back. "Are you coming, or not?" she said. "These fifty elves probably aren't going to volunteer."

Beneath the hood, the beast grinned a mouthful of razor-sharp teeth.

14

The surgery – for that was what it was, despite its lack of clear signage, broken elevators and just about adequate cleanliness – was almost silent. The lunatic had gone; off to gather more links for his sickening chain, no doubt. He had left the trio (though now, thanks to the beast's adroitness with a sharp knife and a needle and thread, they were a single organism) with an explicit set of rules, and the knowledge that, should they break any of those rules, there would be hell to pay.

Rule One: Don't try to escape. There is no way out, and it would therefore be impossible. A waste of time. Why not sing a song, instead? Or, in the case of Rudolph and Jimbo, hum one?

Rule Two: No Justin Bieber. See Rule One.

Rule Three: Try to keep the screaming to an absolute minimum. This is a very nice neighbourhood, and the last thing people want is an incessant screeching ruining their day.

Rule Four: Try not to move around too much. The stitches are new, and liable to come away should enough force be used. This might sound great to you (yay, freedom!) but I assure you that would not be the case. A very painful few minutes would follow, and then, due to massive blood loss, death. Why not sing a song instead?

Rule Five: No Katy Perry. See Rule One.

They were very clear rules and, since there were only five of them, not too difficult to remember. One would have to be an absolute idiot to disregard them.

"Shall we try to escape?" Sissy said, pushing up onto her elbows.

"Mph!" said Jimbo.

"Pfpfpf," whinnied Rudolph.

"Yes, I know what the lunatic *said*, but we've been here for hours now, and I'm starting to get a

73

little pissed off with the whole thing." She scanned the room, looking for anything that might be of use. The nutter had taken the bag of sharp objects with him. The sharpest things in the room, now, were Rudolph's antlers, and one of those was wedged inside her husband. Still, a tiny light-bulb appeared in the air above her head before disappearing just as quickly. "Rudolph, you're a sentient beast, aren't you? I mean, you know what I'm saying right now, yes?"

"Trtrtrtr," Rudolph said, which was good enough for Sissy.

"How are you at picking locks?"

"Pfffff," said the reindeer, which was not the answer Sissy had been hoping for.

"Typical," Sissy said. "You can fly, and not only that but you can pull a sleigh laden with toys and a clinically obese saint at the same time, but when it comes to sticking your antler in a lock and giving it a little wiggle, you're about as useful as a pair of tits on a fish."

Rudolph shrugged.

"Well, we're just going to have to improvise," Sissy said. "After three, we start walking toward the door. Everyone understand?"

"Mph ermh ermph?" Jimbo asked.

"What are we going to do when we *get* there?" Sissy echoed. "We're going to attempt to get the hell out of here. I'm going to line Rudolph up with the keyhole and, whether he likes it or not, he's going to stick his free antler in it and jiggle until we hear a click. Failing that, we're going to have a little lie down and wait for the maniac to return."

"Mrh mph, o ah mrph t murgh."

"No, it *doesn't* sound like much of a plan," Sissy said, "but it's better than anything either of you have come up with, and don't give me the old 'Oh, we can't suggest anything because our faces have been stitched to arseholes' pretext. I can understand you just fine, so if either of you have any bright ideas, now's the time to speak, or mumble, or whatever…"

Silence, and then Rudolph farted. Sissy didn't envy the poor bastard that was going on the back end of the reindeer.

"So, on the count of three," Sissy said, suddenly glad that she was the one leading this incongruous expedition. "One…two…"

"Mrph whr mpth o thr mph mrhfth thr?"

"Are we going on three or *after* three?" Sissy growled, clearly annoyed with her husband. "It doesn't fucking matter. I'll be surprised if we make it to the door at all."

"Mpth mrhth," Jimbo said. For some reason, he had a terrible headache coming on. He had inhaled a lot of gas…

"Okay. One…two…thr—"

"Ampht ftht."

"What do you mean, you're *stuck*?" Sissy shrieked. "How can you be *stuck* on anything?"

"Fthft mph, Rdlph!" Jimbo said, wiggling his backside.

"Oh!" Sissy said. "Rudolph, be a gent, or a lady, and turn your head to the left so my husband can crawl without you tickling his ribs."

Rudolph sighed, for reindeer are renowned for their lack of tolerance. The reindeer turned its head anyway, lest it never hear the end of it.

"One…two…three!" Sissy edged forwards, Jimbo did the same, and Rudolph, who was trying to wake itself up from this terrible nightmare, followed suit. Before long, they had gathered enough momentum to shift at a decent rate. They were never going to win any medals, but, as the saying goes, 'Slowly, slowly, catchy monkey'. Trouble was, the people who usually said it had never caught a monkey in their life, or even chased one.

"We're halfway there!" Sissy said. "Doing very well!"

"Hrmph!" Jimbo said.

"Out of *breath*?" Sissy said, incredulous. "We've only covered three feet!"

If only, Jimbo thought, *she* was the one in the middle. "Harmph hmph mrth thrm stft!" he said.

"Yes, I *know* you're attached to my bottom, and therefore subsisting on the little air you can suck in through your miniscule nostrils, but that's no excuse to start slacking. We've got an escape to make. Do you really want to be here when that freak comes back? Do you *really* want to get caught trying to escape, when he clearly stated in his list of rules that it was absolutely fruitless and would result in a terrible punishment?"

"Frfthtfrthfth," Rudolph said. *Has she always been like this?*

"Lwyth," Jimbo replied. *Always. To be honest, I don't know why I ever married the old trout.*

"I *am* here, you know," Sissy said. "And I don't appreciate being called an old trout, Jimbo. You might want to watch what falls out of your mouth, because I'm in complete control of what falls in, if you catch my drift."

Jimbi said "!", which was one more punctuation mark than was safe.

"Right!" Sissy said. "To the door, me hearties!" She shuffled slowly forwards, one knee, and then the other, and then...well, you get the idea. Seven minutes later, they were at the door, though Jimbo didn't know that, for he had passed out and was being held up between the other two like some sort of elfish spit-roast.

"Can you reach the hole, Rudolph?" Sissy said across her shoulder.

"Pthpthpth," Rudolph said. *Not without tearing your husband's anus off.*

"Well, try anyway," Sissy said. "I don't know about you, but I've got a funny feeling we're running out of time." The funny feeling she was, in fact, talking about, was a rumbly in her tumbly, an odd tickling sensation on the back of her neck, and a strange burning sensation in her ears. She wasn't to know, but these were all side-effects of the mild sedative the lunatic had injected them with before operating, and not a sign that their abductor was on his way back, which would have been a lot more impressive.

Rudolph took a deep breath and exhaled, which actually inflated Jimbo so that he looked like one of those novelty Garfield balloons. Pushing onto its tendon-less haunches, it reached up for the keyhole with its free antler.

"That's it," Sissy said. "You're almost there." She was, of course, guessing. She couldn't see past her bloated husband.

Rudolph managed to push the smallest part of its crown into the keyhole. There was an audible click, which didn't mean anything, really, but for a moment it gave the reindeer hope.

"Now give it a wiggle," Sissy said. "Pretend you're having a seizure."

The reindeer didn't know what a see-za was, and so just shook its head back and forth repeatedly. Thirty seconds later, the wooden door was a mess, but the lock was still…locked.

"Thrft a mrth anthrg," Jimbo said, yawning.

"Did you miss anything?" Sissy parroted. "Yeah, you missed Rudolph making a right pig's ear of the door. And please don't yawn inside me again. It's awfully off-putting."

Rudolph went at the lock once again. There was no point in being careful any more. If the lunatic came back now, he would see the damaged door and would know that they had ignored Rule One. No, it was time for urgency. Time for more force.

Time to attack the lock with every ounce of its antler.

"What's he doing back there?" Sissy yelled, though she couldn't quite hear herself over the raucous din emanating from the rear. It sounded like Pinocchio was being battered to death by a team of angry Transformers.

"Hth thmtg therder," Jimbo said.

"He's smashing the door?" Sissy said. "Well, tell him to keep it down a bit. There's no need to get all rowdy and trash the place. We're not Mexicans."

Ignoring the whining woman at the front of the grotesque creation, Rudolph managed to force his free antler through the wood. Jimbo moaned as the other antler, the one inside of him, twisted more than a little to the left. He'd never felt so much pain back there, and he'd been an altar-boy elf as a child.

Once Rudolph had a hole to work with, the wood came away pretty easy. Splinters flew across the room. Chipped paint rained down on the two elves. Terracotta was an awful colour for a door, anyway.

Before long, Rudolph had made a hole big enough for its head to fit through, and fit its head through it did, or at least, as much as the attached elf's bottom allowed it to.

"What do you see?" Sissy asked, hardly able to contain her excitement. They were almost out, almost free of this terrible, surgical-cold place, with its raving lunatics and its perpetual supply of butterfly stitches and gauze.

Rudolph looked around. The truth of the matter was, it couldn't see much at all. Everything was dark, and dirty. It was like pushing one's face up against a black shroud. In fact, it was *exactly* like that.

And then the darkness moved, and Rudolph looked up to find the hooded lunatic staring down at it.

Rudolph slowly retracted its head. "Hth thr mrkthd mnyk," it said.

"The dark lunatic has *returned?*" Sissy said, frowning. "Is that some kind of code, like they use in those films with the spies and the...*oh*, the dark lunatic has returned...oh, I *see*. Okay, well, at least we tried. I'm going to pass out now for a while. Night-night."

In the adjacent room, behind the shrouded figure, fifty confused elves – who had been promised decent remuneration for a few hour's work – started to have second thoughts about the whole thing.

15

Snow gently drifted down in the village. Elf children ran about the streets, throwing snowballs and building men from snow, which were aptly known as *snow-men*. The first shift up at the workshop was about to finish, which meant that those elves working nights were getting ready for twelve hours of hard graft. And Finklefoot, who should have been standing in line with the rest of his gang, clock-card in hand, and yet wouldn't for a good few days thanks to piss-poor management and a group of odd disappearances, was severely pissed off.

A snowball slammed into the side of his face, which didn't help matters. He turned, growled at the culpable kids, who in turn ran away, laughing and screaming in equal measure.

"You'd better run, you little fu…" He caught himself there, for it wasn't good form to curse at children. He didn't want to be *that* elf; the one the kids avoided for being a grump. You start off with a growl, and before you know it, the elf-kids are leaving bags of reindeer shit on your doorstep, or scrawling 'Bah, humbug!' on your door in barely legible snow-spray graffiti.

It wasn't the kids' fault, either. What were they expected to do with themselves when their parents were working silly hours at the workshop? The Christmas crèche was at capacity, and there wasn't a school, to speak of, for education was as pointless as a bible at a strip club. You either aspired to work at the workshop, knocking out cheap toys at a rate that most sweatshops would deem cruel, or you applied to work at the liquorice factory, where an eternity of ill treatment at the hands of Hattie Hermann awaited. It was surprising, therefore, that there weren't more deaths by suicide in the teenage elf population.

Trudging through the snow, Finklefoot didn't know what he was looking for, or where his feet were taking him. Just that he was moving, and that moving could only be a *good* thing. The snow was deeper in places than others, which meant he had to be very careful where he stepped. Three times he'd had to drag himself out of a drift with

82

his teeth, while the nearby elf-kids laughed and taunted, no less.

Being Santa's personal PI was not as much fun as it sounded.

Just then, something hissed and crackled on his belt, and then a deep, and yet almost robotic, voice said, *"Feeblefruit, are you there?"*

Finkefoot plucked the Spiderman walkie-talkie from his belt and pushed the button. "It's *Finklefoot*," he said, shaking his head. "And yes, of *course* I'm here. If I *wasn't* here, then where would I be?"

"Ah, very good," said The Fat Bastard. *"I just thought I'd check in. You know? Make sure you haven't been kidnapped, too. I don't have to tell you how much that would affect our investigation."*

"I should imagine it would draw the whole thing to an abrupt end," Finklefoot said. He stopped walking for a moment to admire a very well-crafted snow-llama. It was nice to see some of the elf-kids were thinking outside the box.

"It just occurred to me," said Santa, *"that these disappearances are an inside job."*

"Well, we live in a world set apart from the humans," Finklefoot said, planting his face in his palm. "Of *course* it's an inside job."

"Brilliant!" Santa said. *"This is what I'm paying you for."* Even though he wasn't. Not really. *"So with that in mind, I thought you might want to check in on a*

couple of the old companions. Sounds like something one of them might do, what with them being my dark minions, and whatnot."

Santa's Companions. No two words sent a shiver down Finklefoot's spine quite like those, apart from maybe *anal beads*, or *tax return.* The Companions were as mean as they came. Worse than that; they were so mean, and big, and dark, they made Satan look like a fifteen year-old cheerleader:

Krampus. Perhaps the most famous of The Fat Bastard's henchmen. With horns that would make a billy-goat defecate with fear, and a tongue that would make, well, Gene Simmons defecate with fear, Krampus was never going to win awards for his looks (unless there was a 'See how many post-its you can stake on your horns' competition). Krampus was a mischievous beast, but a kidnapper?

Next up there was Belsnickel, or Dirty-Ass Santa as he was known by the elves. Belsnickel's dark, grimy beard had never once seen a drop of Pantene, and neither had the fur coat he insisted on wearing year-in, year-out, even though the fashion had changed an awful lot since 1101AD. Would he be crazy enough to put himself on The Fat Bastard's naughty list?

Then there was Zwarte Piet, or Black Pete as he was once known. Nowadays, he goes by the name of Not-as-white-as-everyone-else Pete, which was far more PC than the alternative. Pete still wore a curly black wig – he'd made it his own, and if anyone had a problem with that, they could simply go and fornicate themselves – but had tried to tone down on the blacking-up so as not to upset some of the black elves. Was *Pete* behind all this?

Or maybe it was Knecht Ruprecht, Santa's fourth and final companion. Roughly translated as *Farmhand Rupert* (much to his chagrin) Ruprecht was another filthy, bearded sonofabitch. He had a gammy leg, and limped everywhere, which made it highly unlikely he had anything to do with the missing elves and reindeer.

"No," said Finklefoot. As a response, it was a long time coming, but that was the only way to fit the above introductions in.

"*No?*" Santa said. "*What do you mean 'no'?*"

"I *mean*," Finklefoot said, "that I would rather chew my own nutsack off than confront one of your buddies. I'd rather chew *your* nutsack off, and I'm a vegetarian…"

"*Ho-ho-ho! There's nothing to be frightened of,*" The Fat Bastard said, with no conviction whatsoever. "*They're on our side. Well, at least three of them are. The other one, well, you'll find out soon enough. If one of them is responsible, mark my words, they'll rue the day…*"

85

If one of them is *responsible,* Finklefoot thought, *then it'll be* me *rueing the day, for as long as they let me live, anyway.*

"And you don't think this is just a little bit dangerous?" Finklefoot said.

"*Oh, this is batshit* insane," replied Santa, "*but an elf's got to do what an elf's got to do. Be sure to contact me if you find out more.*" And with that, the walkie-talkie hissed incessantly. Santa was gone. Momentarily. Then he popped back to say *'Over and out'* in the voice of The Green Goblin before disappearing again.

Finklefoot stood there with the walkie-talkie in his hand for a good fifteen minutes. It was only when a snowball clobbered him in the back of the head that he came to his senses.

Talk to the Companions?

"I'm going to die today," he said, before kicking the snow-llama over with one brutal swipe of his foot.

*

"What do you mean he's on a mission for The Fat Bastard?" Trixie said. "We're supposed to be watching the last series of *Breaking Bad* tonight on Netflix."

Rat shrugged. Shart opened his mouth to speak, before realising he had nothing worthwhile to say, and Gizzo was too busy hammering pieces of wood together to notice she was even there.

"We're not happy about it, either," Rat said, tossing a six-fingered doll-arm in the reject bin. "He's only gone and agreed for us all to work straight through to Christmas Eve."

"He's *what!?*"

"It's true," Shart said. "I wouldn't mind, but I've left the gas on."

Trixie couldn't believe what she was hearing. She'd known Finklefoot was a *Yes* man when she'd married him, but *this*…well, this was the straw that broke the llama's back. Of course, she wasn't to know that it was her husband's foot that broke the llama's back…

"I'm not standing for this," Trixie said, rolling her sleeves up. "If he shows up here before I get my hands on him, be sure to tell him that if he doesn't come home tonight, he'd better not come home at *all*."

"Do we have to say it in that voice?" asked Rat.

"If it helps," replied Trixie.

"I think it might."

Trixie turned and marched toward the clocking-out machine, where she clocked out three times – hard – before pushing her card into the slot with so much force it ended up looking like an origami swan.

87

In the distance there was an almighty explosion.

"Oops," Shart said. "Don't suppose anyone has a spare room?"

16

The hooded lunatic snorted candy-apple snuff off the back of his hand and growled. Darkness was falling, or would have been if they were anywhere but The Land of Christmas, which meant that it was almost time to return to the streets to gather the next worthy participants. Not that any of them were worthy. All that truly mattered was that they had the necessary holes, and that they didn't put up too much of a struggle.

"Is everyone feeling okay?" the maniac said, suppressing a snort.

"*Hmph!*"

"*Frth!*"

"*Brgh!*"

"*Thrgh!*"

The vowel-free replies went on and on as fifty-two elves and a reindeer scrambled around on the surgery floor, slipping and sliding in blood and pus. At least ten of the elves had fainted, but when you had a convoy of so many, it didn't matter if a few engines faltered. There was barely any room down there on the floor, which was why the lunatic had taken to the table, where he could loom over them more efficiently.

"Look, you've made your point," Sissy said, pushing back against the tide of elves behind her. "Why don't you take a photo and start unpicking us? Huh?"

The beast cackled. "You really are a piece of work, aren't you?" he said. "Such courage, and yet you're only 1.87 percent of my creation. From where I'm standing, you're the only one with an ounce of hope left. You think I've come all this way, put in all this hard work, just to *release* you?"

"That sounds *wonderful*," Sissy said. "Do me first, will you? My back's killing."

The maniac climbed down from the table, finding just enough space on the floor to place his large feet. One brave elf tried to nip at his leg, but only succeeded in nibbling the asshole of the guy in front, who let out a surprised, "Grhhhh," as a result.

"We are not quite finished, yet," the figure explained. "Sure, you look good. Certainly very centipede-y, but the whole point is to create a human *Santa*pede—"

"(In)Human Santapede," Sissy corrected, for she wasn't backing down on that.

"Whatever. The point is, until The Fat Bastard is leading you around The Land of Christmas, I will not stop. I will not relent. I will not WILL YOU STOP TRYING TO BITE ME!?"

"Sorry," Sissy said, spitting out a mouthful of dark shroud. "I couldn't resist." She stopped crawling, forcing everyone else to a halt, and called across her shoulder, "You idiots do know that we don't have to keep moving, don't you?"

"*Hrmph!*"

"*Thrgh!*"

"*Hthrgh!*"

"Good. Then can you all stop nudging me forward. Since I appear to be the spokesperson of this monstrosity, I'd appreciated a little cooperation." She turned back to the menacing figure standing over her. "And what happens when you get Santa? What happens then?"

Beneath the hood, the maniac grinned. "Then *Christmas*, and everything it means to you fools, will be lost forever."

17

Finklefoot stood in front of the huge, gothic mansion, his tiny hand hovering a few inches from the door. The doorknocker was a bronze thingummy in the shape of a giant sack of toys. At least, Finklefoot *hoped* that's what it was. Not that it mattered; the elf was far too small to reach it. Whatever possessed a person to install a doorknocker so high up, especially when ninety-nine percent of the land's inhabitants were elves?

But that was the thing. The owner of this mansion didn't *want* callers; didn't like them. Didn't like *anyone*, really. It was a miracle that there was a doorknocker in the first place, and also that there wasn't an electric fence running around the grounds, and a couple of rabid hounds sitting out front. It was also a miracle that Finklefoot had mustered the courage to approach the mansion. He was either really very brave, or incredibly stupid. Perhaps a little of both…

"*Fangleflop!*" a voice hissed. Finklefoot's heart leapt up into his throat before moving beyond that. He could almost taste the arteries. He snatched the walkie-talkie from his belt and depressed the button. Not depressed the button, as in told it a sad story and called it a hurtful name, but pushed it in.

"Shhhhhh!" the elf gasped. "And don't keep startling me like that. I'm not carrying a change of dungarees. And please get my name right. If I'm going to be your second-in-command, you should be able to remember who I am."

"*Yes, yes, yes,*" Santa said, impatiently. "*Where are you? Right now, at this minute, presently?*"

Finklefoot swallowed his heart back down and said, "I'm about to knock on Belsnickel's door."

He gave the door a cursory glance. "Remember? You said I should speak to the Companions? Why?"

"*Oooooh*," Santa said. "*I bet you're awfully frightened right now, but don't let him intimidate you. At the end of the day he's my second-in-command, and—*"

"Hang on a minute. He's your second-in-command, too? So you have three second-in-commands?"

There was a long crackle as Santa exhaled. "*Technically, I have six second-in-commands, if you're including the Companions, my wife, and yourself, and then, of course, there is Hattie Hermann, which makes seven, and then—*"

"Look, do we have time for all this nonsense?" Finklefoot said. "I'm about to have a heart-attack here, and I'd really rather get this over with so I can get back to the village, preferably in one piece."

"*Ho-Ho-Hold your horses, Finkleflaps,*" Santa said. "*The reason I called. Yes, there was a reason. Your wife, Trixie. She's not best impressed that you're working straight up until Christmas Eve. A couple of your gang reckon she's on the warpath. You might want to keep an eye out for her; I know what elf bitches be like when they gets a bee in their bonnet.*"

"Did you just speak gangsta?"

"*Is that what it was?*" Santa said. "*I thought I was having a stroke.*"

Finklefoot closed his eyes and sighed. Not only was he standing on the porch of one of the most terrifying Companions in The Land of Christmas, but now Trixie was after him, and the longer it went on, the angrier she would get. By the time she caught up to him, she might be carrying an incredibly sharp spear and wearing nothing but a loincloth.

Why can't I just say no when people ask for help?

"*Oh, and I've just had a call from Hattie Hermann,*" Santa went on. "*She reckons that fifty of her elves have gone missing. Just disappeared off the production line. Apparently she's down there right now cleaning up. I don't know much about liquorice, but I imagine it gets quite messy if left unattended.*"

"*Fifty!*" Finklefoot said. "Did you say *fifty*!?"

"*Yes,*" Santa said. "*As in Shades of Grey, Gates of Wisdom, US States, Golden wedding anniversary, the amount of rings you need to transform Sonic to super Sonic in that hedgehog game, the—*"

"I *get* it," Finklefoot said. "But how can that *happen*? I mean, how can fifty elves just vanish like that? We're small, but if you put enough of us together, people are going to start noticing if we just…cease to be there."

"*One would think,*" Santa said. "*Anyway, I think we can safely put these latest disappearances down to our Xmas extremist. On the bright side, it should be easier to find the culprit now.*"

"How so?" Finklefoot removed his hat and scratched his head.

"*Well, like you said,*" Santa said. "*You put enough of you together, it's much easier to notice you.*"

Finklefoot couldn't fault his superior's logic, no matter how hard he tried. "Thanks for the heads up," he said. "If you don't hear from me in ten minutes, Belsnickel has ground me to a fine powder and, no doubt, snorted me."

"*You'll be fine,*" Santa said. "*Just ask the right questions and get the hell out of there.*"

"What are the *right* questions?" Finklefoot said, exasperated. Only the crackle of the walkie-talkie answered. He attached it to his belt and stepped up to the magnificent door.

He knocked.

He waited.

He knocked again.

He panicked.

He farted.

He waited.

He cried a little.

He was about to knock one last time when he discerned movement on the other side. A growl, followed by the click of a latch, and then the door swung inwards to reveal a hulking tower of a man. Covered head-to-toe in fur, and with a face only a mother could love (and even she wasn't too keen on it), Belsnickel was the epitome of creepiness. If one were to bump into him in the dead of night, perhaps in a dark alleyway, one would certainly shat oneself, and if one didn't, then one was a much braver elf than the one standing on Belsnickel's porch.

"Do you have a minute to talk about Jesus Christ?" Finklefoot said, for reasons unbeknownst to him. He'd panicked; pretending to be from the *Society of Elfish Jehova's Witnesses* seemed like a much better option than accusing the big guy of elf-larceny and reindeer-rustling.

The fist that caught Finklefoot on the nose suggested he'd probably made a big mistake.

And then there was darkness. The kind of utter opaqueness that only came from being knocked the fuck out.

18

"Did you *have* to hit him?" a voice boomed.

"Yeah, that was a bit much," added another. "You could probably have just said you were into Satan. They give up pretty quickly once they know you've moved over to the dark side."

"I *panicked*," said a third voice. "I didn't know what to do. He was talking about Christ, and, well, I've always thought the best way to make them stop is with a clobbering to the temple."

Finklefoot was drifting in and out of consciousness. Though he could hear the three voices as they bickered amongst themselves and discussed the best way to dispose of the body, he couldn't see who they belonged to. His vision was hit and miss, with the emphasis on the miss. When his eyes were open everything seemed to swirl together, like one of the kaleidoscopes Rufus cobbled together up at the workshop. *This*, Finklefoot thought, *is what Keith Richards must feel like all of the time…*

"I didn't hit him *that* hard," the third voice said. "He went down awfully easily."

"He's an *elf*," the first voice said. "You're Belsnickel. You could have flicked him and he would have gone over."

"Not-as-white-as-everyone-else Pete is right," said the second voice (presumably, Finklefoot thought, Knecht Ruprecht). "Elves aren't great at taking giant fists to the face."

"Well, they should come with some sort of warning," Belsnickel said.

"What? Like an *elf*-warning?" Knecht Ruprecht said, sniggering. And then there was much merriment and endless witticisms, none of which Finklefoot found funny in the slightest.

"Hang on! He's coming to," said Belsnickel. "See, I *told* you he wasn't dead."

"I'm not dead," Finklefoot said, pushing himself up onto his elbows. He was in some sort of games room. Pushed up against the walls were myriad flashing slot machines and videogames. Across the room was a pool table and bar. A neon sign hanging from the ceiling said 'BELSNICKEL'S – WHAT'LL IT BE?'. "I'll be okay in a minute. I just need to get my bearings…" Though Finklefoot knew that his bearings were the least of his troubles. He was in a room – *Lord* knows where – surrounded by three out of four Companions, each of which glared down at him as if he'd just spat in their beards.

"Look, I'm sorry for punching you upside the head," Belsnickel groaned. "It's just that I'm not very good in social situations, especially with elves I don't know."

Finklefoot climbed to his feet, went down again, climbed to his feet and managed to stay up, thanks to Not-as-white-as-everyone-else Pete's cloak. "That's okay," he said, though it wasn't. He hadn't been punched that hard since Trixie's father found them rutting behind the sleigh-shed. "I don't think there's any permanent damage. I guess I'll find out in a few years' time. You wouldn't happen to know the way to Amarillo, would you?"

"He's confused," Knecht Ruprecht said to his buddies. To Finklefoot, he said, "HOW MANY

97

FINGERS AM I HOLDING UP?" in that way that people do when they're talking to a recently-concussed idiot, or a drunkard, or George W. Bush.

"I'm fine," Finklefoot said. "I just need some fresh air, and…" He paused as his vision cleared for the first time since coming round. That was when he remembered the water-pistol The Fat Bastard had presented him with. He reached down, and was surprised to find it still there, tucked behind his buckle. He didn't want to have use it, but it was nice to know it was there if things turned ugly, or if he should suddenly grow a pair…

There, on the table the Companions were seated around, was a deck of playing cards. Stacks of chips were neatly aligned in front of each player, along with their respective hands. In the centre of the table, a bowl of pretzels looked mighty inviting. Bottles of brandy and sherry stood next to half-empty glasses.

"Am I interrupting a poker match?" Finklefoot asked. He didn't know much about poker, but the way the cards had been dealt, it was clear they weren't playing *Snap!*.

"You could say that," Not-as-white-as-everyone-else Pete said, lighting a cigar that was almost the same size as the elf. "We like to get together every few weeks, play a few hands, smoke some stogies and drink some spirits. It gets us in the mood for Christmas."

"Yeah, it's the only thing that keeps us sane in the run-up to the big day," Belsnickel said. Leaning back in his chair, he poured himself a very large Brandy. "You can only get *so* excited about handing out shitty gifts to naughty kids."

"Santa's got it *easy* compared to us," Knecht Ruprecht said, forcing a handful of pretzels into his mouth. "He gets all the good kids, the ones who've been nice. I get to deliver sticks and coal to little shits. And if those little shits are still little shits next year, I get to beat them with the stick."

"I hand out *stings* to bad children for a living," Belsnickel said. "Do you have any idea how degrading that is? Stings? I mean, who's afraid of a little sting these days?"

"It must be really tough for you," Finklefoot said. But he wasn't interested in their traditions; he was more interested in the poker game. "How long have you been playing?" he asked, gesturing to the large table.

The Companions exchanged confused glances. God, there was a lot of facial hair in the room.

"How long has this particular session been going on?" Knecht Ruprecht said. "Or how long since we started getting together for drinks and cards?"

"The *first* one," Finklefoot said. For some reason, he was no longer frightened. It probably had something to do with the fact he was still slightly concussed. No *sane* elf would stand around conversing with seventy-five percent of the Companions. *In a moment*, he thought, *I'll come to my senses and run for the door.* Until his legs started to function again, though, he had no choice but to natter. While they were talking to him, they weren't thumping him in the head, which could only be a good thing.

"About three days," Knecht Ruprecht said, as if that was a perfectly normal answer. "We like to make an event of it. Drag it out for as long as possible. Like B said; it's the only thing that stops us from going mental before Christmas Eve."

Interesting, Finklefoot thought. *Three days…they've been playing cards for three days…together, which puts the Companions in the clear…*

Or at least *three* of them.

"And Krampus would normally be *here* with you?" For the first time, Finklefoot felt like he was in control. He wished he had a brown mac and a glass eye, so he could act all confused, even though he knew damn well what was going on.

"Hasn't missed a poker session for centuries," Not-as-white-as-everyone-else Pete said, slamming down a glass of brandy as if they were going out of fashion. "And then, all of a sudden, he sends Belsnickel a letter. Something about a head cold. Personally, I think he's just scared. We took him for two million candy canes last year, and I don't think he's got over it."

Finklefoot walked across the room, to where Belsnickel had perched himself on a stool next to the bar. He picked up a bottle without checking what it was first – it was one of those days where *anything* alcoholic would do, including turps and surgical spirit – and took a deep gulp. Once the burn subsided, and once he managed to peel his lips away from his teeth, Finklefoot said. "Did Krampus mention anything to you boys about ruining Christmas?"

Glances were exchanged, most of them confused.

"All the time," Belsnickel finally said. "It's kind of his thing."

"Remember that time," Knecht Ruprecht laughed, "when he was going to swap all the toys in the sleigh for reindeer shit?"

Not-as-white-as-everyone-else Pete and Belsnickel sniggered in unison. The room palpably shook. "And that year he was going to lace The Fat Bastard's mince pies with Rohypnol." They were laughing so hard now that, to an elf (and therefore to Finklefoot), it was slightly terrifying.

"What about that Christmas he fucked Mrs Claus, and then tried to blackmail her with the sex tape?" Belsnickel snorted.

"Forgot to press record on the hidden camera, didn't he?" Knecht Ruprecht said, laughing so hard that he was leaking gas. "Oh, Krampus! He's a card."

At some point, Finklefoot had joined in with the laughter. Wiping tears from his eyes, he said, "So, he's always banging on about it, is he?" he said. "Ruining Christmas, and all that malarkey?"

"Oh, god, yes," Belsnickel said, filling his face with peanuts from the glass bowl sitting atop the bar. "I mean, we all *talk* about it, but Krampus... well, he's a maniac."

Interesting, Finklefoot thought, for the second time in as many minutes.

"Not that he'd ever *do* anything, really," Knecht Ruprecht said, stroking his beard. "He's a lot of talk, and very little walk." Though he didn't sound as convinced as he might have wanted to...

Finklefoot was on to something. He could feel it in his stumpy little bones. And his scalp tingled, but that might have just been the fleas he'd contracted from one of the many beards in the room.

"Where," Finklefoot said, "might I find Krampus, if, say, I wanted to have a little natter to him about something?" *That's the way to do it*, he thought (though for some reason it sounded high-pitched and nasally). Keep it loose and obscure. The less these three giants monsters knew about what was going on, the better.

"You really don't want to go bothering Krampus this close to Christmas," Belsnickel growled. "Especially if he's feeling under the weather. I mean, you wouldn't go tickling a polar bear with a feather, would you?"

"Wouldn't *dream* of it," Finklefoot said. "But just humour me. For future reference, as it were, where might I find the one known as Krampus?"

The three Companions sighed in unison. Suddenly, the air tasted stale, and extremely flammable.

"Do you know where that new takeaway mince-pie shop is over on Festive Avenue?" Not-as-white-as-everyone-else Pete said.

"*Pie on the Fly?*" Finklefoot said. "Yeah, I know it."

"Well, if you take a right from there, you'll come to a small blue house."

"Blue house," Finklefoot repeated. He wished he was writing this down.

"Now, all the houses in The Land of Christmas look the same, as you already know, but this one's blue, and it's the only blue one down that way."

"Gotcha." *Blue house*, Finklefoot thought. *How hard can it be?*

"From the blue house, you're going to want to take a few steps back. I can see you've only got little baby feet, so twenty good steps ought to do it."

A map had formed in Finklefoot's head, and he thought he knew the place well enough to say, "Hang on. Won't that put me on in the frozen river?"

"Yes, which is a much better place for you to go than looking for Krampus."

All three of them laughed. Finklefoot didn't, at least not at first, not until he remembered he was in the company of three Companions.

"That's wonderful!" he lied, making his way toward the door. "The way I fell for that…man, I'm an *idiot*. Okay, well, I guess I'm not going to get anything more than that…ah, what a blast! We really must do this again some time."

"Sorry I hit you so hard," Belsnickel said, wiping drool from his beard.

"Oh, *that*! I've forgotten all about that already." Which might have also been a side-effect of being hit so hard. He turned, reached for the doorknob, and paused… as pauses went, this one was dramatic. The kind of intense pause you get when someone farts in an elevator.

"There is just one more thing," Finklefoot said, turning back to the room. What he would have given for a half-chewed cigar...

The Companions quietened down and regarded Finklefoot with something akin to interest.

"Can I use your toilet before I go? I'm bosting for a piss."

19

It was a Civil twilight, which meant that the sun had set only a few degrees below the horizon, and not that it went around being overly nice to everyone. Because of the perpetual brightness, elves could continue their day as if nothing had changed, which was all fine and dandy for most of them, but it played havoc with the lives of the night-watchmen.

"I don't know why *I* had to come along," Mrs Claus said, pinching her nose between thumb and forefinger. It was cold in the stable, and her nipples had stiffened beneath her red and white brassiere. It was something, Santa thought, to hang his tools on if his arm grew tired. "You've never needed my help mucking out the reindeer before."

Santa straightened up. The shit piled on the end of his shovel slipped off, hitting the stable floor with a meaty thump. "I'm not letting you out of my *sight*, dear," he said. "Not until we've figured out what's going on around here." He scooped up the shit and carried it across the stable, to where a large, black bag sat open on the floor. "I mean, this kidnapper of ours might be a *rapist*," he continued, shaking the shit off the shovel. He said the last word as if it burned his tongue. "How would you like *that*? Huh? Get dragged off to some basement where you'd be fingered, fucked and buggered to within an inch of your life?"

Jessica Claus's eyes lit up for a moment. But then it struck her that the perpetrator might be of the...*tall* variety, and any stirrings she felt quickly dissipated.

"No, until we've caught this monster, it's best that you don't leave my side." Santa scooped up another mound of deer shit (Blitzen's – he knew that curvature anywhere) and transported it to the bag.

Mrs Claus shivered. No-one had the bollocks to tell her she would be much warmer if she didn't walk around the place like a half-naked coquette. "Do you really believe that dumb elf of yours is going to get to the bottom of this mess?"

"Fluglefang isn't *dumb*," Santa reproached. "He's just a little…what's the word?"

"*Little?*" Mrs Claus said.

"No. He's the right elf for the job," Santa said. "You'll see. He'll figure out what's happening around here, and then—"

Just then, something thunked into Santa's neck. He dropped the shit-laden shovel and slapped his hand over the affected area. There was something there – a projectile of some sort – and when he pulled it free, he saw that it was a dart. On its flight was the internationally-recognised symbol for 'you're about to have a very bad fucking day', or the skull and crossbones, as it's more commonly known.

"What is it?" Mrs Claus asked, stepping toward her husband and the miniature thingamabob he held in his hand. "Is that a *dart?*"

Suddenly, Mrs Claus screeched. Her eyes widened and her mouth fell open to reveal an already swollen tongue. She reached around and yanked something from her ass, which turned out to be another dart, identical to the one Santa had just pulled from his neck.

"What'th going on," she said, though her tongue was inflating at an incredible rate. She knew those would be her last words for a while.

Santa dropped to his knees, though not in despair. He just couldn't control his legs any more. Luckily, as a fat man, he had plenty of padding over his kneecaps, and so didn't do too much damage. The wooden floor beneath him, however, splintered immediately, spiderwebbed out to where eight nervous reindeer watched with absolute fascination. "I think we've been poithoned," he said. "The dartth…thereth thomething in the dartth." He dropped the dart, with its none-too-friendly flight, and watched as it rolled across the stable floor, coming to a halt only when it met a giant, black boot.

Mrs Claus joined her husband on the floor, completely paralysed. She landed awkwardly – one boob out, the other pushed up against her left ear – and, no matter how hard she tried, she couldn't roll over to see why The Fat Bastard's eyes were so wide, his mouth trembling with horror, his frown so deep.

"No," Santa said. "Thith can't be—"

"Well it *is*, you fat sonofabitch," a voice growled. Mrs Claus thought she recognised it, but her tongue had become so distended in her mouth that everything sounded…*wrong*. "How are my drugs working for you? Hm?"

Santa dropped to the left, like a toppled statue, and remained there, inert and ineffectual. "Thatuthiththu," he said, though even *he* didn't know what it was meant to be.

"Just relax," the voice hissed as it circled the fallen Clauses. "You're going to start feeling very sleepy, and when you wake up...ooh, when you wake up, you're going to be so impressed with what I've been working on."

Santa's eyes rolled into the back of his head. He was losing it, losing touch with reality, which was a remarkable state of affairs given what he did for a living. The dart's contents, whatever the hell they were, had reduced him to a slobbering, slumbering wreck in less than twenty seconds.

"You should feel *honoured*," the voice said, though it was fuzzy now, as if it was coming to them through several gallons of water. "This is going to make one hell of a Christmas card, one for all the family, one that can be treasured year after year..."

Santa huffed. It was almost impossible to breathe, now. Just then, the walkie-talkie on his buckle hissed and crackled, and then the voice of his second-in-command (or at least one of them) came through loud and clear.

"*I think it's Krampus!*" the voice said.

"He thinks it's *me!*" Krampus said, leaning down and snatching the walkie-talkie from The Fat Bastard's belt. "Who is this?" he said, speaking into the walkie-talkie.

There was a slight pause – as Krampus had anticipated – and then a tiny, shaky voice said, "*Who is* this?"

Krampus sighed. He'd played a lot of tedious games in his lifetime, including the week-long poker tournaments with the rest of the Companions, but *this* game…this game was never going to take off the same way, say, Monopoly had.

"I asked you *first*," Krampus said, watching as Santa and Mrs Claus drifted slowly, and inexorably, into unconsciousness. Krampus had time to wonder if Mrs Claus was cold in her get-up before the small, timorous voice said:

"*Can you put The Fat Bastard on, please? I promise, I'm not trying to sell anything.*"

Krampus laughed, and it was a terrible laugh. It was the kind of laugh one associates with Bond villains and tax-dodging politicians; the kind of laugh that created gooseflesh out of thin air. "Your boss is…how should I put it…? Otherwise engaged." Krampus pressed another button on the walkie-talkie, for he was not to be trusted with buttons of any shape or size. "What does this one do?" he said.

"*Oh, you've pushed the Green Goblin button,*" the voice said. "*You might not be able to hear it at your end, but you sound just like the…you know what? It doesn't matter. What do you mean by 'otherwise engaged'?"*

Krampus, proving once again that he was nothing if not capable of multi-tasking, dropped Santa Claus's feet. "I mean," he said, "that he can't come to the phone right now because he's a little bit unconscious."

Silence...

More silence...

A crackle, and then a soupcon of nothingness, before the voice returned. "*Krampus,*" he said. It wasn't a question.

Krampus had hogtied Mrs Claus – and not just because she liked it – and was dragging her across to the open sack he'd laid out on the floor. "You're remarkably good at this. I'm looking for a few good elves. How would you like to be part of something truly unique?"

"*I wouldn't,*" said the voice. "*What have you done with them all? What have you done with Rudolph? And Santa?*"

Krampus stuffed The Fat Bastard into a sack (it was a very large sack, the heavy-duty kind you use for garden waste) and pulled the drawstring, cutting off his pudgy captive's snoring, or at least muting it a little. "Don't worry," Krampus said. "Nobody is dead yet." Maybe, once the reindeer pushed out a shit, that would all change...

"Why are you doing this? This is The Land of Christmas. People don't go around kidnapping other people. We're not Mexicans."

"Are we still using that joke?"

"Can you think of a better one?"

As a matter of fact, Krampus *couldn't*. And why should he? It wasn't his job to come up with such things. Instead, he slung the two sacks across his shoulder – needless to say, one of them was a helluva lot heavier than the other, meaning he walked with a lopsided gait, and almost ended up in with the remaining reindeer.

"What are you going to do with them?" the voice asked. *"It's not Christmas policy to negotiate with terrorists."* Not that there was any government in place to spearhead such negotiations. Whoever had set up the system all those years ago really hadn't put much thought into it, at all.

"I'm going to stitch them together," Krampus said. "I'm going to stitch them arse to mouth so that they are one long, singular organism. It's what shall be forever known as...The Human Santapede." He sniggered as he said it. Such a great name...such a brilliant idea...

There was a pause; Krampus could almost hear miniature cogs rotating as his fellow communicator turned the information over in his head. *"Wouldn't it be an* Inhuman *Santapede?"* the voice cropped up. "*I mean, if you wanted to be* really *pedantic about it.*"

"I'm toying with the idea of brackets," Krampus said. "I don't know how it will…look, it doesn't matter. What *matters* is that this Christmas is not going to happen. 2014 will be the year of the Krampus, and the year that Santa shat into the faces of those that revere him so foolishly."

"*But don't you see!*" the voice pleaded, "*that by killing Christmas, you are, in fact, killing yourself? Don't you have homes to visit, too? Children to disappoint and terrify? Without Christmas, you are nothing…all of us…we're nothing!*"

Krampus trundled away from the stables, his cargo swinging behind him like Adolf's ball-bag. "*You* will be nothing," he hissed into the walkie-talkie. "*I* will be the creator of The Human Santapede—"

"*Yeah, I'm not feeling that name at all. What does it sound like with brackets?*"

"Look, I don't have time for this," Krampus said. "It's snowing like a motherfucker again, and I'm carrying a fat saint and his whore-devil wife—"

"*You've got Jessica, too!?*" the voice gasped.

"Of *course* I have," Krampus said. "When I came up with the idea of sewing hundreds of elves together, she was the first thing I thought of. Funny that, isn't it?"

113

"Not really." The voice sounded bored, now, as if its owner had a million-and-one things it would rather have been doing than conversing with a maniacal Companion. *"You'll never get away with this, Krampus, and even if you do, you'll never work in this town again!"*

Krampus sighed. "Promises, promises," he slithered. "Well, must dash. These mouths and arseholes aren't going to stitch themselves together." And with that, he dropped the Spiderman walkie-talkie and crushed it beneath one heavy boot. Two would have just been overkill...

He whistled a tuneless ditty – nothing remotely Christmas-y – and went about his work like the consummate professional he was turning out to be.

*

Finklefoot stared down at the walkie-talkie in the only way he could: as if it had just called him a dirty midget. Krampus was behind the disappearances, and now he had The Fat Bastard and Mrs Claus.

He was going to do horrific things to them. Things that only a sick mind could come up with. A Human Santapede? A string of grotesque, malformed elves all sewn together to form one gruesome creature…?

"Well this," Finklefoot said, shaking his head and trying his damnedest not to pass out, "is a bit of a clusterfuck."

As understatements went, it was up there with *Mumbai is not the cheapest place in the world to live* and *Cannibalism is frowned upon in most societies.*

20

The workshop had come to a grinding halt as far as work was concerned, which was always the case whenever Santa and his wife left the building. A couple of the braver elves had ventured outside for a quick smoke, while a couple of the more suicidal elves were up in The Fat Bastard's office, raiding his brandy supply. Bodies – some partially inebriated – ambled aimlessly from one station to another, striking up conversation with whoever would listen. It was a rare occurrence, and one that might not be repeated this side of the big day, and so it was no surprise that people were making the most of it. How did the old adage go? *A change is as good as a rest?* Well, the workshop had certainly changed in the hour or so since Santa's departure, so much so that several of the elves had fallen asleep at their tables.

"Shall I change the music?" Gizzo shouted down from the first-floor mezzanine. His question was answered with a thousand sighed yeses. After eighteen-thousand repetitions, *any* song is bound to get on your nerves.

"Won't Santa know we were in his office if we change the music?" Rat asked, and a damn fine question it was, too.

"Are you kidding me?" Gizzo said. "He's been at the sherry all day. He wouldn't know if we changed the tape to *Metallica.*" He rushed across the landing and slipped into The Fat Bastard's office. Rat followed, as rats are wont to do, and watched as his colleague located the boom-box and switched the tape. After a moment of hissing, the opening chords to Bobby Helms' *Jingle Bell Rock* seeped out through the speakers across the workshop, much to the satisfaction of the workers below. It wouldn't last. Come next year, they would be screaming out for a different song.

"Come on," Rat said. "If we get caught in here, he'll have our guts for garters. This time tomorrow, we'll be dressed as leprechauns in the human world, selling marshmallow cereal in some overcrowded shopping mall."

Gizzo shrugged. "You say that like it's a bad thing." They walked out onto the mezzanine and down the steps. "My great-grandfather was a leprechaun for years. Says it was the best thing that ever happened to him, and he doesn't even like green."

Rat was about to retort when he noticed a kerfuffle amongst the workers. Someone was pushing through the crowd, tearing their way through the sea of half-drunken elves to get to…*them*?

"Is that *Finklefoot*?" Gizzo said.

Rat nodded. "Eager to get back at it, I suppose," he said. "You know what he gets like when he's away from his station for too long." They had once watched their foreman squeeze three shifts into two, just to please The Fat Bastard. It was little wonder that Finklefoot had very few friends, inside and outside of the workshop. Joseph Fritzl had more buddies than Finklefoot, and the way he was careening through the half-cut elves, he'd have even less by the end of the day.

Rat and Gizzo arrived back at their station a few seconds before Finklefoot. Shart was putting the finishing touches to an extremely unattractive doll. It was, Shart thought, the kind of doll that serial killers possessed to enact vengeance upon the humans that ended their killing spree.

Finklefoot gasped for air. He was plastered with snow and, as it melted, steam rose up all around him. It took him quite a while to get his words out, and when he did, the three members of his gang wished he hadn't bothered.

"What do you *mean*, 'Santa's been kidnapped'?" Shart said, popping the final leg into the hideous doll's socket. "This isn't Mex—"

"Can we not do the Mexico joke again?" Finklefoot interrupted. "Once is fine, but now we're starting to sound racist."

"We wouldn't want to come across as racist," Rat said. "I mean, we're not Irish."

"So, why would anyone kidnap Santa?" Gizzo said, removing his little green hat and scratching at the bald patch beneath.

"It's *Krampus*," Finklefoot said, staring down at the ghastly doll in Shart's hand. "Is that thing *meant* to look like that?"

Shart nodded. "I think so." Though it did look extraordinarily creepy, but wasn't that true of some newborn kids? Most, in fact.

"Why would Krampus kidnap The Fat Bastard?" Rat asked.

"Keep your voice down," Finklefoot whispered. "The last thing we need is unnecessary panic. You see, it's not just Santa that's been abducted. Krampus has Jessica, too, and Rudolph, as well as fifty of Hattie Hermann's lot…"

"Holy *shit*!" Shart said. "That's baaaaaaaad!"

It *was* bad, but it would be far worse if the rest of the workshop found out about it. Many of them had relatives over at the liquorice factory. Finklefoot knew for sure that Ahora's sister worked there, rolling up the Catherine wheels. There would be chaos if news got out that Krampus had lost his mind and intended to surgically attach elf, reindeer, and fat saint to form a Human Santapede.

"He's going to stitch them all together," Finklefoot said, grimacing at the very thought of such irreverent behaviour.

"To make some sort of (In)Human Santapede?" Shart said, frowning.

"Oh, so *that's* what the brackets sound like," Finklefoot said. "Yeah, that's *exactly* what he's going to do. I don't know what's pushed Krampus over the edge, but he's determined to ruin Christmas this year, and it's up to us to stop him."

There was a collective sigh as Shart, Rat, and Gizzo looked at anything that wasn't their foreman. To make eye-contact was to accept that they'd heard him, and that was just…*silly.*

"Boys, I can't do this on my *own*," Finklefoot said, giving the last word a syllable or two more than it required. "If Christmas doesn't happen, that's *it* for us. It's not like Valentine's Day. We can't just miss a year and hope that no-one

119

notices. If Krampus succeeds, The Land of Christmas will shrivel up like a dick in an ice-bath. And then, when it's all shrivelled and small, it will vanish completely. If you hadn't noticed, there's more than a bit of magic swirling around here, and what do you think will happen to that magic if Christmas doesn't happen?"

Shart shrugged. "I'm thinking 'nothing good'," he said.

"Exactly. Who *knows* what will become of us. Perhaps we'll just cease to exist, like Amelia Earheart or that kid actor from *ET*. Maybe we'll explode, or implode, or *both* at the same time."

"Maybe we'll go to heaven and be given seventy virgins a piece," Rat said, smiling slightly.

"Don't be ridiculous," Finklefoot said. "This is The Land of Christmas, not fucking Narnia. Besides, how many elf virgins do *you* know?"

"We *are* an incredibly horny race," Shart said. "I'm horny right now." He glanced down at the ugly doll he'd been working on a moment ago. Horny? Yes. Desperate? No.

"The point is," Finklefoot said, trying to remember if there was one, "that if we don't do something to stop Krampus, everything we know and love is going to suffer. We've all had our issues with The Fat Bastard over the years, but does he deserve *this*? Does Jessica Claus deserve *this*?"

Shart glanced at Rat, who turned to Gizzo, who in turn simply shrugged. "I don't suppose we're going to get danger-pay for this?" he said.

"Or *pay*?" Shart added.

"We'll get so much more than pay," Finklefoot said. "We'll be revered across the Land. We'll be celebrated wherever we go. We'll be treated like royalty." He hoped that last part wasn't true, for the stories he'd heard about royalty always culminated in a jolly good beheading.

"We want a song," Shart said, straightening up. "Something that'll be played every Christmas in the human world. And Elton John has to write it, and it has to start playing in malls across America in October; that way it gets three whole months, which is plenty long enough to become embedded in consumers' heads for the rest of their lives."

Finklefoot smiled. "I'm sure that can be arranged," he said. "And if Elton can't do it, I'll get Barry Gibb."

"As long as he doesn't *sing* it," Rat said. "We want it to be catchy, but not annoying."

"So, do we have a deal?" Finklefoot regarded each of his gang with optimism. "You boys going to help save Christmas, rescue The Fat Bastard, and put an end to Krampus's madcap plan?"

"Like we've got anything better to do," Gizzo said.

"Just give me five minutes," Shart said, running for the toilet block and pulling at his dungarees zipper as he went. "I wasn't lying when I said I was horny."

𝔄

"*You better watch out…you better not cry…*" Krampus sang as he pushed the needle through Mrs Claus's oral mucosa and into the fleshy meat of The Fat Bastard's ass for the umpteenth time. "*You better not pout…I'm telling you why…*" He laughed, then bit through the thread. "*Santa Claus is coming to town…*NOT!"

He stood and took a few steps back, so that he could take it all in.

"Remarkable," he said. "Absolutely splendid." He walked along one side of the creature, occasionally kicking out at a panicking elf, and then down the other side. "Better than I could have ever imagined it," he said. The grin beneath his hood was now a perpetual thing, and not just a fluke.

It was finished. The Human Santapede – (In)Human Santapede, if you were an obfuscator, and it turned out that there were more of them out there than Krampus could ever have anticipated – was complete. Krampus couldn't believe he'd done it; he'd actually done it. No more talk, no more beating around the proverbial bush. He was the only Companion with the bollocks to pull something like this off, and he couldn't wait to show them his creation in all its grotesque glory.

Just then, from the very front of the organism, a gruff and tired voice said, "Ho-Ho-Holy fuck, my ass is sore."

Krampus danced – for he was in a fantastic mood, and didn't care a pip that he looked like a drunken swan – along the Santapede, smacking Jessica Claus's derriere as he passed her. She squeaked, but nothing more. She hadn't quite come to, yet. Unlike her husband, who was now shaking his head and trying to figure out why his legs refused to do as he wished.

"Ahhhhh!" Krampus said as he moved around the front of the creature. "You're awake! And not a moment too soon!"

"I should have *known* YOU had something to do with all of this," Santa said through gritted teeth. "But what I don't understand is *why*? Is this because I'm better than you in practically every way? *Is it*? Is it because I get to wear the red and white while you have to walk around wrapped in black, like some Goth Buddhist? Is it because my beard is always so clean, and yours…well, yours looks like something you would pull from Gandalf's plughole?"

Krampus's dark and demonic face shrivelled up as if he'd just sucked on an overly-ripe lemon. The Fat Bastard really knew how to push his buttons. Even now, on his knees and ass-to-mouth with his beloved Jessica, his mouth ran away with him. It was terribly frustrating for Krampus, who was hoping for tears and pleas.

"I see you're still a little mouthy," Krampus said, walking across the cold, damp room, to where a bottle sat upon a trestle table. He picked up the bottle and grinned. "Maybe I should have put you halfway down the line. Though I doubt even thirty second-hand shits would silence the likes of you."

Santa shuddered at the thought. "You're making a big mistake," he said, though he had a feeling it was too late. Krampus had gone too far, and when people go too far, they tend to see only one way out, and that's by going just a little bit further…

"*Am* I?" Krampus said. Santa figured it was entirely rhetorical, and not something he should even deign to answer. "This has been coming for centuries, you chubby cunt. People will only take so much, and you…you've finally overstepped the mark."

Santa frowned. He had no idea what he'd done to invoke such madness, especially from one of his own. "What if I were to offer you a role as my second-in-command?" It was a long shot, but there didn't appear to be any short shots available to him.

Krampus prowled across the room, stooping just in front of Santa's face. "You would do that for me? Make me your *deputy*?" He fluttered his dark red eyelashes with mock elatedness and growled. "You must think I'm a fucking idiot."

"I—"

"I've spent the last god knows how many millennia helping you, taking care of the little shits that you can't be bothered with, and for what? You must think I was born yesterday. All that sherry's gone to your head, you daft old twat."

Santa was about to speak when a glass bottle was thrust into his open mouth. The liquid – whatever it was – caught him by surprise, and before he had a chance to close his throat-hole, half the bottle was on its way to his stomach. Gasping for air, and drooling what remained of the acrid fluid into his beard, Santa said, "What…what was…that…?"

Krampus began to read the bottle, as if even *he* wasn't certain. "It says here that it's LaxiMax. I'll let you figure out the rest."

Santa gawped in horror. "You...you *evil...*!"

"Yes, yes, we've already established that," Krampus said, tapping the bottle with his right horn. "Now, if I were you, I'd try to relax. It'll help with the...well, everything'll just run smoother if you don't talk."

"You sonofab..." was as far as The Fat Bastard got before his stomach began to roll. He grunted.

"Works faster than I thought," Krampus said, investigating the empty bottle. "I'll buy this one again. It says it's a "number two bestseller" but I think that's just a joke."

"Oh-oh-oh," Santa said, closing his eyes.

Behind him, his wife, a reindeer, and fifty-odd elves all whined in unison.

22

The four elves stood in front of the huge mansion, staring at one another, their eyes filled with fear and trepidation, their hearts pounding faster than Ron Jeremy on speed. None of them knew what they were doing; just that it was so ridiculous that it might just work.

"Is that doorknocker a *scrotum*?" Shart asked, pointing up at the bronze thingamajig.

Finklefoot shrugged and removed the water-pistol from his belt. "This is probably going to go south really quick," he said. It was four against three, technically, but they were elves, and the Companions were bloody great big muscular things with veins on the outside and masculine beards. In essence, it was like pitting a quartet of mice against a trio of pit-bulls.

"You're absolutely right," Rat said. "So why don't we cut out the middle-man, the bit where we're attacked and beaten to within an inch of our lives, and throw ourselves out onto the street now? We wouldn't even have to knock the door."

"No, we have to try," Finklefoot said. "Besides, I have *this*." He held up the water-pistol for the others to see. Unsurprisingly, it didn't elicit a collective cheer of relief.

"Well why didn't you *say* so?" Shart said, his voice drenched with sarcasm. "Everyone, relax. Our fearless leader is packing. And you've all heard the stories about how much the Companions hate water, especially when it's leaking toward them in a singular jet at 5 miles-per-hour."

Finklefoot sighed. "It's not an *ordinary* water-pistol," he said, though it sure did look like one. "The Fat Bastard gave it to me. It was in his safe."

"Were there other things in his safe?" Gizzo asked. "Like those little snapper things that go *BANG!* when you throw them down?"

"Oh, you're talking about nuclear warheads," Shart said, smiling. "Now *those* we could use."

"Look," Finklefoot said, trying to remain calm. "Just *trust* me. I've got this. And leave the talking to me. Things could get very confusing if we all start prattling on."

"Hey, this is your show," Shart said, taking a step back. "Do you want a leg-up so you can reach the bronze ball-bag?"

Turning to the door, Finklefoot took a deep breath and hammered as hard as he could with the barrel of the water-pistol (that he hoped *wasn't* a water-pistol). Behind him, there were rustlings and mutterings as his elven cohorts fought the urge to run away as quickly as possible.

"Come on, come on," Finklefoot whispered. *It would be just our luck if they've gone off for a game of late-night golf,* he thought. He cast his mind back to earlier that day; saw the myriad empty bottles lined up on the bar, on the poker-table, on the floor. There was a very good chance they were, all three, comatose.

A rumbling on the other side of the door extinguished any hope that the Companions had drunk themselves into a stupor. Finklefoot tensed up; his bones audibly cracked. His bowels relaxed; his trousers audibly squeaked.

The door thunked.

The door opened.

A beard appeared in the crack, above which sat a pair of baffled – and slightly glassy – eyes. The door began to shut again.

Then there was an almighty explosion of blue light, and the door flew backwards, leaving its hinges attached to the doorframe. Belsnickel became very small very quickly as he soared back into the mansion, his legs kicking out as they left the ground, possibly for the first time since he was born…

It all happened so quickly, and yet in super slow-motion at the same time, which was a little disconcerting for the four elves watching from the hole in the front of the building. It wasn't until Belsnickel slammed into the wall at the end of the hallway – toppling a rather fetching watercolour portrait of himself in the process – that things seemed to speed up again. And then it was sheer madness.

Knecht Ruprecht and Not-as-white-as-everyone-else Pete appeared in the hallway, still cradling their respective poker hands, as if they still didn't trust Belsnickel, despite the fact he was all-but splattered against the far wall. For a moment, neither of them saw the assembly of elves standing in what used to be a very nice doorway, and then followed the trail of debris, and it was only a matter of time before…

"It's that fucking Jehova's Witness elf!" Knecht Ruprecht cried. "And he's got The Fat Bastard's Anti-Companion Water-Pistol™!" They both lunged for cover, disappearing from the hallway and landing with a thump in the living room. The whole house shook. A chandelier fell from the ceiling and landed on the already-battered Belsnickel.

Finklefoot, who was still holding the smoking water-pistol (a miracle, really, considering what it had done to the mansion's frontage), swallowed hard. He turned around to find Shart, Rat, and Gizzo cowering in a bush. Either that or the force of the blast had sent them backwards.

Turning back to the smouldering hole, Finklefoot said, "That was an accident. I'm more than happy to pay for any damage. I know this elf, McFeegle? Did a *great* job on my bathroom." Ah, who was he kidding? That was the single-most exhilarating thing he'd ever done in his life. It was a pity he hadn't meant it.

"What do you *want?*" a voice – *Knecht Ruprecht*, Finklefoot thought – said. Gone was the sonorous, menacing tone; it had been replaced by a quivering, terrified whine. The kind of voice

Finklefoot felt comfortable with, since they were on the same level.

"You can't *kill* us!" Not-as-white-as-everyone-else Pete said. "The Fat Bastard wouldn't allow it!"

"Will you lot get out of that shrub," Finklefoot whispered back to his gang. "Honestly, you give an elf an inch and they try to take a yard." To the gloomy, smoky hallway, he said, "We're not here to kill *anyone*. We need your help. Like I told you earlier, something terrible is happening in The Land of Christmas. Something that could ruin us. *All* of us."

There was a moment's silence, and then Knecht Ruprecht said, "Put the Anti-Companion Water-Pistol™ away and we'll talk."

Finklefoot thought about it, and was about to replace the weapon when sense made a brief appearance. The water-pistol had just made the Companion's mansion open plan; the last thing he wanted to do was push it back down his waistband, where it might go off, thusly taking off his bottom half and leaving him even shorter than he already was.

"I've got nowhere to put it," he said, looking around for somewhere suitable to stow it, if only for a few minutes. "Don't suppose either of you owns a holster? Only I quite like my knackers."

"Point it at the floor," Knecht Ruprecht said. "We're coming out."

"Well this is going better than expected." Shart said, pulling leaves and twigs from his pointy, green hat. "Thank the Lord for itchy trigger fingers."

Knecht Ruprecht and Not-as-white-as-everyone-else Pete appeared in the hallway, and slowly walked toward the hole, their hands raised. Behind them, Belsnickel stirred, but that was all he did.

"I didn't mean to shoot him," Finklefoot said. "It just went *off*."

"Just keep it pointed at the ground," Knecht Ruprecht said. "Sheesh, The Fat Bastard gave you *that*?"

Finklefoot nodded. "I thought he was taking the piss. I didn't even know what it was, but now it makes perfect sense."

"It also makes perfect holes in ancient architecture," Rat said, running a stubby finger over the edge of the aperture. "I'm very impressed. Can I hold it for a bit?"

Ignoring his colleague, Finklefoot said, "The Fat Bastard's in danger. Krampus has kidnapped him, and plans to make him into some abhorrent creature—"

"He's a fat man with a beard who drinks a lot and sneaks into houses in the dead of night, leaving soot and chimney-jizz all over the place before raiding the fridge," Not-as-white-as-everyone-else Pete said. "How could he be made any more 'abhorrent'?"

"*Wait*," Knecht Ruprecht said. "Krampus has *kidnapped* The Fat Bastard?" He shook his head. "He finally did it. He finally went full-on Gary Busey whacko. I thought it was a little weird how he couldn't join us for poker. 'Head cold' my arse."

"It's not just Santa he's abducted," Finklefoot said. "He's got Jessica, too. And Rudolph, not to mention fifty of Hattie Hermann's lot."

"Ah, he's going to make a Human Santapede out of them," Knecht Ruprecht said without even flinching.

"You *knew* about this?" Finklefoot was shocked, and yet why should he be? Why should *anything* shock him anymore?

"He'd mentioned it," Knecht Ruprecht said. "We just thought he was batshit crazy. Never thought he would actually go *through* with it. Plus, we had this whole discussion about whether it should be *Inhuman* Santapede, or even with brackets…"

Finklefoot had, for some reason or other, the sudden urge to shoot the still-conscious Companions where they stood, if only for shits and giggles. "Well, he *did* it, and we can't stop him without your help."

"Sounds like you're doing a good job so far," Not-as-white-as-everyone-else Pete said. "To be honest, I don't fancy getting involved in all this. It sounds awfully messy."

"It'll be a lot messier if we don't do something about it," Shart said. "Finklefoot's done the maths. If we don't stop Krampus, The Land of Christmas and all its contents will fall apart quicker than a jealous swingers orgy."

Knecht Ruprecht bunched his mouth up on the one side, the way people do when they're considering something tricky. "So what you're saying is that we don't really have a choice in the matter."

"Oh, you *have* a choice," Finklefoot said. "It all depends on whether the thought of vanishing in a mist of utter agony sounds appealing to you."

"So what you're saying is that we don't really have a choice in the matter," Not-as-white-as-anyone-else Pete reiterated.

"If you want to put it that way," Finklefoot said. "Then yes, that's exactly what I'm saying."

Knecht Ruprecht sighed. "Fair enough." He turned and gestured to the mess at the end of the hallway, a mess that had, not too long ago, punched Finklefoot in the head. "We'll just wait for Frank Bruno to wake up and we'll get a wriggle on."

Finklefoot sighed with relief; a gesture echoed by his fellow elves.

Not-as-white-as-everyone-else Pete leaned against the ruined doorframe. "Do you think they'll write a song about us?"

"You know," Finklefoot said. "They'd bloody better."

23

Santa shook his head as his stomach continued to roll. Behind him, Mrs Claus choked and sobbed, and behind her, Sissy and Jimbo coughed and spluttered. Rudolph knew what was coming, and was thinking happy thoughts (*Raindrops on roses and whiskers on kittens. Bright copper kettles with warm woollen mittens. Brown paper packages tied up with strings*, etc. etc.) but it was no use. It was almost impossible to concentrate on anything *but* the kerfuffle taking place at the front of the monstrosity, of which Rudolph was very much a part. *If I just keep my tongue here…*

At the back of the Santapede, several of the elves were swaying from side to side, trying to break free of the madness, but to no avail. You could say what you wanted about Krampus – at least, you could if your mouth wasn't stitched to somebody's asshole – but you couldn't say he wasn't thorough. The sutures were excellent. No matter how hard the elves pulled, they couldn't break away. It had left at least ten of them with broken jaws.

Krampus sat on a swivel chair at the front of the room, putting the finishing touches to his parade map. He couldn't decide whether it was best to take a right at the liquorice factory, so that those on shift got a good look at their humiliated workmates, or to take a left, down past the stables. It was, he thought, a real pickle.

There was only one thing for it. He picked up the phone and dialled.

"Ah, Hattie," he said, far too gleefully for the circumstances. "Yes, yes, they're being very well-behaved…yes, they know not to piss me off…what's *that*? No I did not know about Trigger's asthma." He put one taloned hand over the receiver and turned to the Santapede. "Which one of you is Trigger?"

About halfway along the creature, a small, stumpy arm reached for the air. Krampus smiled, satisfied that the elf's asthma hadn't ruined his creation. The last thing he needed was a weak link.

"He's *fine*," Krampus said to the receiver. "I don't know how long that'll last, but for now, he's still breathing, though I bet he wishes he wasn't." He laughed evilly. "You'll have to excuse me. I haven't had this much fun since ACDC Donnington '92. Anyway, the reason I was ringing…yes, of *course* they'll all be back at work tomorrow." It was a lie, but lying wasn't the worst thing he'd done that day. "Could you bring the rest of your staff to the village in about an hour, only I think you're going to want to see this…yes…yes…an hour and half, then? Yes, I *know* how busy you are, but…" Krampus was losing his cool. "Okay, let me put it another way. If you are not in the village in an hour, then I'm going to come down there and feed you all into your little confectionary mixers, how does that sound?…Oh, you will? That's marvellous. Thank you for being so accommodating. I will see you in an hour." He dropped the phone back into its cradle and leaned back in his chair. It was a silly thing to do, since there was no back on it.

Picking himself up from the cold, hard ground, he made eye contact with The Fat Bastard. "What are you looking at, Tubby?"

"Why?" Santa said, groggily. "Just *why*?" He looked like a defeated man; exactly how one might imagine the head of a meaty, shitty snake to look. He had the same expression that politicians get when they're found to be fiddling their taxes.

"Why?" Krampus said, dusting himself down. "Why, why, why? Well, there are *lots* of reasons, really. Do you remember the time you belittled me in front of the other Companions for putting too much coal in children's socks? Made me feel about as big as one of your elves, you did. And what about the time you decided to dock me a year's privileges?"

"You can't go…around…kicking elves…in the face…" Santa said. "It's…*rude*…"

"Yes, well, we wouldn't want to be *rude* to your precious elves, now, would we?" He snorted. "But the icing on the cake, the straw that broke the camel's back, the final stroke, the match in the powder barrel—"

Santa farted. "Is this going…to take long…?"

"—the nail in the coffin, the *colpo di grazia*, was when I lent you my MaxBlower3000 and never got it back."

Sometimes, you hear something so ridiculous that simple speech becomes impossible. In that moment, Santa couldn't find any words, at least none that made sense. Then, of course, there was the chore of putting them in some sort of coherent order. In the end, he decided not to bother.

"That's *right*," Krampus said. "You remember? About twenty-five years ago, you came to me and asked if you could borrow my snowblower. I said,

'Yes, of course, my dear friend. It's in the shed, behind the coal-sacks, next to the lawnmower that never gets used'. Off you went, merry as always, belly shaking like a condom full of blancmange; off to deprive me of the only snowblower I possessed. If I'd known I would never see it again, I would have at least took the time to wish it all the best for the future…"

"This…" Santa said, incredulous. "All of this…is because of a snowblower?"

"Not just *any* snowblower," Krampus corrected him. "A MaxBlower3000. *My* MaxBlower3000. Do you have any idea how many sleepless nights I've had over that snowblower? Do you know how many times I've cried myself to sleep, yearning for the feel of it in my hand once again?"

"You've got to be *shitting* me?" Santa checked the corners of the room, looking for hidden cameras, for this had to be some ill-conceived prank.

Krampus straightened up. Santa was grateful; the Companion's breath was disagreeable to the point of being offensive. "I wouldn't expect you to understand, you rotund rascal," he sneered. "You're the man that has it all, and what you don't have, your elves are only too happy to build it for you. You're like a fat Richard Branson."

Now that, Santa thought, *is not fair*. He only had one aircraft, and it ran on magic, not the souls of virgins. "The snowblower is…" He tried to remember what he'd done with it. Twenty-five years was a long time, even in The Land of Christmas, where days dissolved into one another like antacids in water. "Well, it's somewhere up at the workshop. I can have eight-hundred elves looking for it within the hour. All you have to do is let us go."

Krampus shook his head and clicked his tongue. Never a good sign. "This isn't about the snowblower anymore," he said, though it sort of was. Just thinking about it – its duel motor, and the sweet, sweet noise it made when it started up – brought a tear to the corner of his eye. "This is about making a point. It's about standing up and being counted. Unfortunately, you can't stand up, which means I win."

"Yes, yes, you win," Santa said, just as his bowels unloaded once again. Behind him, Jessica Claus squealed and sobbed. Her diet had gone right up the Swanee. "You've made your point. I don't think any of us will ever forget what's happened here today. And…" His stomach growled, and he grunted. "…I'll make a public apology. I'll pull out all the stops…I'll—"

"You'll *suffer*," Krampus said. "And you'll do it on your knees, where you belong. For far too long you've been ruler of this land. Not anymore. Things are going to change around here, and by change I mean *come to an end*. You will spend what little time you have left walking around the village, leading my Santapede wherever it takes you, and I shall watch and laugh and enjoy every sick second of it." As if to show how he intended to laugh, he laughed. It wasn't quite what Santa had expected.

"But if Christmas doesn't happen," Santa said, "we will *all* cease to exist. *You* will cease to exist."

Krampus nonchalantly shrugged. "Small price to pay to prove a point," he said. "Unlike you, I don't enjoy Christmas the same way I used to. Maybe I've grown out of it. Maybe I'm just tired. Maybe – and this is just a theory – I couldn't give a shit whether kids have been bad or good. It's not like we have anything to do with them for the other three-hundred and sixty-four days a year. Even the good ones have the capacity to grow up into serial killers."

"Are you still banging on…about Dahmer?" Santa gritted his teeth as his body racked with pain. "That was fifty *years* ago."

"You gave him a plastic barbecue kit and a box of disembodied dolls!" Krampus said. "Don't you feel a little bit responsible?"

Lifting a weary hand, Santa groaned. "Look…we do our jobs…that's all…we can do."

Why should he feel bad? In 1947 he'd gifted Lee Harvey Oswald a toy rifle. How was he to know that the guy would grow up into a Grade A whacko? In 1980, he'd hand-delivered a typewriter to Stephanie Meyer. Was it his fault that she'd gone on to pen shitty sparkly vampire novels? *If you thought like that*, Santa opined, *you'd never give presents to anyone…*

"Well, this time next week you can thank me," Krampus said. "You won't have to do your job anymore. None of us will. No more Christmas. No more petulant children. No more anything. Doesn't that sound absolutely delightful?"

For a moment, The Fat Bastard had to admit that it *did*. No more early mornings. No more Bond film repeats. No more Cliff Richard. It sounded positively wonderful. The only downside would be the fading out of all existence. "Without Christmas, the humans will tear each other apart!" Santa found a little strength from…somewhere. He pushed himself upwards.

"Athethrethuth!" Mrs Claus screeched, grabbing her husband by his love-handles and dragging him back to ground.

"Sorry, love," Santa said. "Got a little bit carried away." To Krampus he said, "You won't just be killing us. You'll be massacring the humans, too. They won't be able to *survive* without the hope that Christmas brings."

142

"Hadn't thought about it like that," Krampus said, his bottom lip protruding slightly. "That's a cheeky bonus. Never could stand those gits, with their sense of annual entitlement. Well, we don't owe them anything. And if they go under just because they wake up on Christmas morning to find the tree bereft of presents, well so be it."

Santa couldn't believe what he was hearing. *This*, he thought, *is what madness sounds like*. Actually, madness sounded like dolphins mating, but this was close enough…

"Now, if you would keep your thoughts to yourself for a while," Krampus said, unhooking what looked like a dog leash from a hook on the wall. "We're going to get ready for a little walk. Put on a brave face…no, not that one…that's a despondent face…try this." He smiled and arched his eyebrows. Santa began to cry, much to Krampus's chagrin. "Oh, well. I suppose that'll have to do."

He stepped toward The Fat Bastard, the leash clinking and clanking in his almost demonic grasp.

This can't be real, Santa thought. *This is too ridiculous to be happening…*

As an ancient and magical saint, tasked with delivering billions of presents across seven continents in less than eight hours – including the umpteen service station stops – the irony was not lost on him.

24

Heavy snow once again blanketed the village, kept at a reasonable depth thanks only to the sudden footfall of hundreds of intrigued elves. Lights strung from lampposts and houses blinked red, and yellow, and green, and white, and…lots of other colours that you're probably already familiar with. *Jingle Bell Rock* drifted down from the workshop for the fifty-eighth time, and yet no-one seemed to mind.

Something *big* was afoot.

Something exciting.

Lining both sides of the street, the elves chuntered on amongst themselves. They were just grateful to get out of the liquorice factory, if only for an hour. The fact that none of them knew why Hattie Hermann had led them down to the village, as if on some sort of field trip (but without the tagalong parents), didn't seem to matter.

"I heard it was the great Ronnie Corbett," one elf said, somewhat optimistically.

"What? The little fella?" said another. From an elf, that was rich.

"I heard we were all going to get a bonus," a pudgy elf with a beard that could choke a donkey added. "That The Fat Bastard's finally come to his senses, that he's realised, all of a sudden, that he's essentially running a sweatshop."

"Nah," said a female elf, who was knitting and therefore not really taking part in the conversation; not wholly, anyhow. "The only bonus we're gonna get is extra shifts. I've been on since *shit…*" She'd dropped a stitch, and everyone knows that dropped stitches are the cancer of the patchwork quilt world. "Three o'clock this morning," she finally said. "If that ain't bad enough, ten of the elves from my section pissed off this afternoon. Didn't even tell Hattie where they were going, or how long they would be. I wouldn't want to be in their shoes when they come back."

"Why? Did they have small feet?" A clever, and yet nondescript, elf said.

"Well, *whatever's* going on," the knitter said. "They need to hurry up about it, or I'll be able to use my nipples to finish this scarf."

Just then, a horn sounded, causing several elves to jump, and at least one to topple back into the snow, clutching at his chest and saying, "Gahrrrrrrrrrr!"

"Aye aye," the knitter said, tucking her needlework away for a later date. "Looks like the show's about to start."

As cheers went up all around the village, a strange atmosphere settled over the land. It was as if one person had left the gas on and everyone else was too stubborn to do anything about it.

The horn sounded again, and this time...

*

"What was *that*?" Shart asked, pushing his way through a snowdrift. Only the top of his hat was visible, but it was a very *nice* hat. It was his going out hat, which seemed apt since he was, in fact, out.

"It sounded like a *horn*," Belsnickel said. He, and the other Companions, were faring much better in the snow, proving once and for all that height is often a great commodity when used in the correct manner. "Does anybody know what goes *heeeeeerrrrrrrnk*!?"

"There are rumours," Rat said, stroking at his chin as if what he was saying would have some major effect on the history of the world. It wouldn't, "that the human female mammary makes such a sound when squeezed in exactly the right place. Of course, I have been wrong before..."

"Oh *good*," Finklefoot said, punching snow aside with duel fists. "You can add that one to the pile, then."

The horn *hernked!* again. *That must be some mammary*, Rat thought.

"It's coming from over there," Knecht Ruprecht said, pointing across to their right.

"No, you're wrong," Not-as-white-as-everyone-else Pete said. "It came from over *there*." He extended a finger in the complete opposite direction. "And I believe it is the same noise a sperm whale makes when its blowhole is plugged up with a rolled-up copy of the Yellow Pages."

"*Yes!*" Belsnickel agreed. "That's what I thought it was, too."

Finklefoot stopped walking and turned to face the lagging Companions. It was strange to think that a few hours ago he wouldn't have dared talk to them the way he was about to. It was amazing the difference an Anti-Companion Water-Pistol™ could make.

"Will you stop talking nonsense and just pick us up," he said. "Gizzo, Rat, you go on Knecht Ruprecht. Shart, climb onto Black Pete's—"

"*Whoa, whoa, whoa!*" Not-as-white-as-everyone-else Pete said. His mouth had fallen wide open. A robin – cute little thing with a red breast, just like on the cards you get from those family members you don't really get on with – landed on his listless bottom jaw before fluttering away again.

"Shit!" Finklefoot said. "Sorry. My bad. It's just a lot quicker to say Black Pe—"

"He said it again!" Belsnickel gasped. "Holy fuck! What is this? 1922?"

Finklefoot felt about a foot tall, which was not far off the truth. "Look, I wasn't being racist. I mean, yes, we were still stitching golliwogs until the late nineties, but does that put me on the same chart as Mel Gibson?"

"It kinda does," Not-as-white-as-everyone-else Pete said. "Do some of your sentences start with 'I'm not racist, but…'?"

"It's very rare," Rat said, which didn't help matters.

"Can we just concentrate on the matter in hand?" Finklefoot said. "We're all about to be expunged from existence, and you lot are yattering on about bollocks. I'm an elf. Do you hear me complaining? No, because that's the hand I was dealt." He moved around to Belsnickel's back and launched himself upwards, grappling for the Companion's waist. Belsnickel, sensing the elf had bitten off more than he could chew, dropped to one knee and helped the poor sod to mount.

The other elves clambered onto their respective rides. Knecht Ruprecht had one on each shoulder, clinging to his beard for dear life.

The horn sounded again. *Herrrrrrnk!*

"Onwards!" Finklefoot said, pointing toward the source of the noise with the Anti-Companion Water-Pistol™ and kicking Belsnickel's side, hard and just above the ribs. The Companion growled. "Sorry," Finklefoot said.

"That's okay," Belsnickel grunted, mainly because the pistol that had almost blown him to smithereens back at the mansion was brushing against his temple. The elf could have called Belsnickel's mother all the names under the sun, and he would have had to agree.

"Let's go save Christmas," Shart said. "For what it's worth."

The Companions marched forwards, their riders terrified and excited and slightly underdressed for what was shaping up to be a battle of epic proportions. Dungarees and pointy hats were no substitutes for chainmail and helmets when it came to war. They would have been safer heading down to the village in their birthday suits. At least then they would have the shock factor on their side.

Heeeerrrrrrrr…

*

…rrrrrrrrk!

"I wish they'd knock that off," said an elderly elf as he adjusted his hearing-aid. "There's no need for it. When I were a lad, this place was quiet. You could 'ave 'eard a gnat fart from miles away…" His little diatribe went on and on, but nobody was listening. They were too busy jostling for a better position, for the street was now filled with boisterous elves. They'd come from all over the village, and news of the mystery show must have reached the workshop. The Fat Bastard's elves came a-rolling down the hill, asking anyone and everyone what was going on and what that bleeding racket was. The air was filled with anticipation, and intrigue, and more than a little confusion, as The Land of Christmas came to a grinding halt, and nobody knew why.

"I haven't been this excited since Uncle Verne visited," a young elf called Udo Troyer said.

"I haven't been this excited since they announced dress-down-Fridays," said another, whose name was not important, nor necessary.

"Ladies and Gentlemen!" a chirpy, and yet guttural, robotic voice said. "I would like to thank each and every one of you for coming! Though, not many of you had a choice in the matter. Am I right? I'm right."

"He's *right*," said one elf, who would rather have been at home with a mug of Horlicks and a slice of Battenberg than standing out in the street, rubbing her bits and bobs together just to stay warm. But Hattie Hermann had made it very clear that any elves not in attendance would be dealt with in the strictest of fashions. 'And I don't just mean a week in solitude,' the confectionary-loving slave-driver had said. Most of the elves knew exactly what she'd meant.

Strawberry lace lashes. Lots of them.

"What you are about to see will disgust you. It will *amaze* you, but mostly it will just disgust you. It will inspire you, but there's a good chance you'll be too disgusted to see it as anything other than an abomination. You will be dumfounded, and disgusted, and hopefully you will be disgusted, and horrified, but mainly just disgusted, and a little bit saddened and angered, and also, of course, disgusted."

There were mumblings from the crowd as they continued to speculate upon the nature of the evening's entertainment. One elf reckoned Meat Loaf was about to burst from one of the houses – like a bat out of hell – and start working through his repertoire of quasi-romantic rock ballads, but that was just wishful thinking, for that elf sure did idolise Meat Loaf…

"You're all, no doubt, wondering what has become of your guv'nor. Hm? And I'm almost certain that a lot of you are concerned about the wellbeing of his wife, the delectable and slightly sullied Jessica Claus? Well, let me be the one to tell you that they are both doing fine. As are the missing elves from the liquorice factory, and Rudolph? How could anyone forget about Rudolph, with his nose so bright, and all that tomfoolery? Yes, they are all alive, and...well, you will see for yourselves in just a moment."

The crowd applauded. So far, it was a good show. Much better than the time David Blaine came to entertain the masses. Three days encased in a block of ice was not so impressive in The Land of Christmas, where you didn't have to walk to the end of your street to see a fellow elf in the exact same predicament.

"Can I request that flash photography be kept to a minimum?" the automaton loudhailer voice continued. "And that nobody attempts to stroke or *feed* the...special guest...as it moves through the village?"

The spectators all nodded in unison. *No flash, no feed.* Even they couldn't fuck that up. As if to prove them wrong, there was a second of bright light before someone called out an apology.

"Elves of The Land of Christmas...I give you..."

"He's milking this for all it's worth, innee?" said a disgruntled voice from the crowd.

"…The Human Santapede!"

What happened in those next thirty seconds would go down in history, which wasn't saying a lot since there might not be a lot of present left to convert to history. But the elves gathered in the centre of the village weren't to know that.

A hooded figure appeared at the end of the street, a loudhailer in one hand and a leash in the other. It was what was on the end of the leash, though, that caused the audience to gasp in horror, and at least thirty of them to swoon. Ahora of the jigsaw puzzle section vomited into her own hands before sinking into the snow, squealing like a caged chinchilla. Mop MaChitup passed out so hard that the elves standing around her had no choice but to follow suit. Blinker and Brewster – the only conjoined twins in The Land of Christmas – tried to run away, but Blinker went one way, and Brewster the other, which meant they didn't get as far as either of them had hoped.

"It's *ghastly*!" one upchucking elf screeched.

"It's a *monster*!" added another.

"Surely it should be called The *Inhuman* Santapede," said a third.

"At least with *brackets*," concurred a fourth.

It was chaos. Utter bedlam as elves attempted to put as much distance between themselves and the aberration as they could. A few of the more...*opportunistic* elves saw it as the perfect excuse to loot, and were therefore running along the street with stolen goods twice their size. One elf slipped on the snow and landed on his back with a *thump*. The fifty-two inch plasma screen he'd been carrying landed on his front with more or less the same sound effect.

"What has become of our beloved leader?" Ahora said, pulling her face from the vomity snow.

"He's been made into a *beast*!" someone yelled, leaping over her and almost taking her hat clean off. "A *beast*, I tell you!"

"I don't think my heart can take it!" one of Hattie Hermann's liquorice workers said. A moment later, he clutched his chest. "Nope. I was right," he said, before falling back into the snow.

And the grotesque Santapede kept coming, dragged through the streets by the hooded lunatic, who was laughing and cackling and, in a fashion, *dancing*. "Where are you all going?" the maniac said, his voice amplified by the loudhailer. "This is what you all came to see." He gestured to the creature beside him and kicked Santa in what would have been the ribs had The Fat Bastard not had fifty inches of blubber in front of them.

"I'll *never* shake the image!" One elf cried before leaping to his death from the roof of his house. A second later, his head appeared in the deep snow nestled up against his frontage. "Bollocks," he said.

Eight reindeer were smoking and nattering amongst themselves when the Santapede ambled past the stables. Blitzen almost choked on his Marlboro, while Donner and Prancer set about resuscitating Dasher.

"I always knew he'd show his true colours," Vixen said, nonchalantly flicking a hoof toward Rudolph. "You can always tell, can't you? One minute they're showing off with their great big red noses, the next…well, just *look* at it…"

The reindeer all turned just as the bloody, battered elf in front of Rudolph began to glow red.

"He's still showing off now, look," Blitzen said, shaking his head. "Yeah, you keep on glowing, you red-nosed prick! Honestly, that's what happens when some asshole writes a song about you."

The Human Santapede continued along the street, leaving a trail of faeces in its wake. The poor elf at the back had passed out, but that didn't stop *things* from falling from his backside.

There were fifty-one elves, a reindeer, and the Clauses in front of him, and all of them had done a little *something* in the past twenty-four hours. Trying to hold one poo in can be deadly, but fifty-one – plus his own – was just suicide.

"Please!" Santa sobbed. "Please can we stop now!?"

"Mthththtsth?" Mrs Claus said, which was more or less what her husband had just asked.

"Oh, no," Krampus said, merrily jigging along the pavement. "We're not going to stop. We may *never* stop. Let us keep going until the snow ceases to fall from the sky and the trees turn green, and Robbie Williams finally comes out as gay."

"But those things will *never* happen!" Santa cried. "At least let us get off the street, to someplace my elves can't see me. Ho-Ho-*Hostel* wasn't even this graphic."

"You should have thought about that before you came knocking my door and asked to borrow my snowblower." Krampus grinned, and it was one of those wide ones; an ear-to-ear grin; a shark's grin; a grin so wide that it stretched all the way around his face and met at the back of his head. Everything above his mouth should have – if we're being pernickety – fallen off.

Krampus reached into his cloak pocket (yes, it had three pockets, one for spare change, one for his cell-phone, and one for his horn, which was all well and good, but where was he supposed to put his receipts?) and pulled out the horn. To his lips it went.

Heeeeerrrrrrnk!!! It was so loud that it required three exclamation marks. *Heeeeerrrrrrrrnk!!!* Even he didn't know why he'd blown it a second time. "Come on," he said, yanking Santa forwards with an unceremonious tug of the leash. "To the village centre we must return. Hattie Hermann's put the kettle on, and I'm gasping."

"You'll go to *Hell…*for this," Santa said, his body racked with pain and sobs.

"Possibly," Krampus said. "But not before I've had a cup of tea and a jammie dodger."

25

The three Companions that weren't raving madmen raced into the village proper, their riders more breathless than they were. The village was almost deserted; nobody had wanted to stick around for any longer than was necessary. Sure, a couple of intrigued perverts loitered about, but for the most part, the elves had dispersed, returning to their homes where there was a much better chance of surviving until morning.

To one of the dallying miscreants, Finklefoot said, "Hello there!"

The perv, whose name was Sid, suddenly looked very sheepish. "A'right," he said.

"Have you seen a Human Santapede? About seventy foot long? Ugly as sin, with The Fat Bastard at the front?"

Sid nodded wildly. "Oh, yes. I've seen it alright. It's the weirdest thing I ever did lay my eyes upon, and I once stood at the front of a Miley Cyrus concert."

Finklefoot climbed down from his steed, though Belsnickel would have refuted such a name, and anyone silly enough to call him it to his face would have perished before they'd had chance to take another breath. "Which way did it go?" Finklefoot said, glancing both ways down the street.

"Last I saw it was headed toward the stables," Sid said. "I'm 'oping it comes back this way. I'd love to see it again, just one last time before we start dying to death."

"Was he armed?" Belsnickel grunted. His breath was visible in the cold air. It was also so pungent that, if you had a butter knife, you could have sliced it clean in half.

"Was *who* armed?" Sid asked. It was a stupid question, but Sid had never professed at being anything *but* stupid.

Knecht Ruprecht took a few steps forwards. "Krampus," he said. "The lunatic. The guy that stitched everyone together. Was he armed?"

Sid frowned. He couldn't remember seeing any weapons on the shrouded man. But that was the thing with concealed weapons; you didn't know about them until they'd been unconcealed. "He had the beast on a leash," he said. "But I don't think you could call it a weapon. If Santa had been growling instead of crying like a baby, maybe—"

"Okay, so he's *unarmed*," Not-as-white-as-everyone-else Pete said, his voice saturated with relief. "Shouldn't take us too long to bring him down."

"He's still the strongest one out of all of us," Knecht Ruprecht said. "We need to be very careful about…"

Heeeeerrrrrrrrrrrnk!!!

Everyone panicked. Rat and Gizzo fell backwards off Knecht Ruprecht's shoulders and landed, luckily for them, in the snow. Shart shuffled further up Not-as-white-as-everyone-else Pete's back and buried himself in the Companion's afro. Finklefoot pointed the Anti-Companion Water-Pistol™ into the gloomy nothingness, turning and turning, hoping to see just a hint of movement so that he could unleash hell.

Sid, the not-so-secret pervert, staggered forwards in the snow. His eyes had rolled up into his head, and he was reaching around for his back as if it was trying to get away from him.

Finklefoot moved to the side just in time as Sid continued forwards. Momentum can be a terrible thing, despite what the great Byzantine philosopher Philoponus said. More people had been killed by momentum than by choking on boiled sweets or autoerotic asphyxiation. The best way to avoid death by momentum was to avoid steep cliffs, railways stations, horseracing events, wild buffalo, and One Direction concerts.

Sid landed face-down in the snow, his legs crumpled up behind him as if they were suddenly independent to the rest of him. The miniature spear embedded in his back was still doinging from side to side, as was its wont…

"Christ on a broomstick!" Finklefoot said, glancing around, searching the semi-darkness for the perpetrator. He didn't have to look far, for a moment later the shrouded figure stepped from the shadows looking particularly smug. The leash in his hand chinked and clinked as he dragged the Santapede from the gloom.

"Blimey, that was a good shot!" Krampus said, removing his hood. "I thought I was going to need a couple of go's at it."

"Shoot him!" Belsnickel roared.

It took an awful long time for Finklefoot to realise the Companion was talking to him, by which time it was far too late. Krampus had crouched down beside Santa and had the horn pressed to his temple, his mouth hovering just an inch away.

"Ah-ah," Krampus said. "I wouldn't do that if I were you. Not unless you want to see your beloved saint's brains spattered across the snow."

Finklefoot sighed. Why did nothing ever go as planned around here? "You kill The Fat Bastard," he said. "You kill us all."

"So people keep telling me," Krampus said, straightening up and yet keeping the horn trained upon the sobbing head of his ghastly creation. The dart – like the one that had just dropped Sid like a sack of mouldy spuds – could be discerned at the end of the horn as its tip protruded ever-so-slightly.

Poison, Finklefoot thought. There was no way such a small dart could do so much damage unless it had been dipped in something mortally astringent.

"Have you lost your mind, Krampus?" Belsnickel said, his voice as deep and serious as ever. "This is no way to behave. This is The Land of Christmas, and we are a peaceful people."

"What does that even mean?" Krampus said, shaking his head. "A peaceful people? Why not just say 'peaceful people'?"

"You're one to talk about misuse of language," Knecht Ruprecht said. "This is the first time I've seen your monster, and it's clearly inhuman. You're lucky you haven't been sued for false advertising."

"It should at least be bracketed," Not-as-white-as-everyone-else Pete said. "Like those Meat Loaf songs."

Krampus waved a hand dismissively. "Whatever. The point is that I've grown tired of all this…this *bullshit*. We work all year round, and for what? One lousy day. And we don't even get the fucking *credit*! No, the kids stopped believing in us years ago. And the parents don't even bother to correct little Jimmy when he gets up on Christmas morning and thanks them for all his gifts. No, they pat him on his little ginger head and say, 'Oh, you're welcome, son. We've worked ever so hard to pay for all these wonderful things, but you deserve them, son, even though you're ginger. You deserve them all', and *that*, my Companion friends, is what has become of your beloved Christmas. *That* is why I'm doing this. Well, that and the fact that this fat bastard doesn't know what the word 'borrow' means." He kicked Santa once in the face. Blood dripped from his nostrils and soaked into his moustache, giving it a pinkish tinge.

"They still believe in us," Belsnickel said, though he didn't sound convinced. "Santa Claus will never die, and nor will we."

Krampus sneered. "That's where you're wrong," he said. "We will all die tonight. Every last one of us."

"He's a bit of a *buzzkill*, innee?" Rat whispered to no-one in particular.

"You can't *kill* Christmas," Knecht Ruprecht said. Suddenly, he looked a lot taller than he had been a moment before. Beneath the snow – of which there was now several feet – and out of sight, Knecht Ruprecht had pushed himself onto his tippy-toes.

"If that's true," Krampus said, "then how come I'm about to blow a hole in The Fat Bastard's head? I mean, if he is the One, then in the next few seconds there has to be some kind of miracle to stop me. How can he be the One if he's dead?"

"Isn't that a line from *The Matrix*?" Shart said.

"Yeah, it's the bit where the evil bald guy's pulling the plug," Krampus said. "But it works here, too."

Just then, there was a metallic clank and Krampus's head snapped forwards. A saucepan landed in the snow just in front of Finklefoot as Krampus tottered unsteadily on his feet.

"Hey, I recognise these porridge burns," Finklefoot said, picking up the saucepan/missile.

"*Frewzerth*," Krampus drooled, fingering the egg that had pushed up through his scalp, making it look like he had three horns. Now, 'frewzerth' wasn't any word in the Oxford English Dictionary, but in The Collins Dictionary of Concussed Ramblings, it meant: (Verb) – Hurt like a sonofabitch…

"Isn't that your missus?" Shart said, pointing to the darkness just beyond the still-staggering Krampus.

Finklefoot squinted. "Well, I'll be damned."

Trixie emerged from the shadows, her arms folded sternly across her chest, her eyebrows knitted together with utter fury. "When were you going to tell me you were working straight through until Christmas Eve?" she said. "I'm only your *wife*. Do I not have the right to know these things? Do we not *discuss* matters anymore? Hm?"

"Can we talk about this later," Finklefoot said, shrinking into his own body.

"Everyone, run for it!" Santa bellowed, clawing his way through the snow at roughly one mile an hour. The rest of the Santapede followed, not that they had much choice in the matter.

Belsnickel lunged for the dazed Krampus, who, despite his current giddiness, dodged to the right. Belsnickel went down in the snow, and the snow went up in the air.

"I've got him!" Knecht Ruprecht said, diving after the escaping madman. Krampus turned and blew through his horn. Knecht Ruprecht flew back into the night as the miniature spear thumped into his shoulder. Lying on his back, staring up at the stars, he said, "Could somebody else get him? I'm gonna have a little nap."

"Finklefoot!" Shart said as he leapt up onto Krampus's trailing leg. "Shoot him with your thingamabob!"

Finklefoot spun, forgetting for the time being that his wife was terribly annoyed with him. Levelling the Anti-Companion Water-Pistol™ at Krampus, he said, "Yippee-ki-yay, motherlicker!" and pulled the trigger.

One minute, Krampus was there, the next there was nothing but smoke and a purple haze.

"You got him!" Shart called from what sounded like a mile away. "Oh, no, hang on. He's back up. He's picking me up and…yep, he's going to throw me."

All eyes turned to the sky just in time to see Shart surge past. "Wheeeeeee!" he screamed. He was like a firework, but without the mess. He smashed through a window halfway down the street, and an alarm began wailing into the night.

"Where did he go?" Finklefoot said.

"Over *there*," Santa said, ambling past with about as much pace as a blind chess tournament.

"Grthsthrh," Jessica Claus mumbled as she clawed through the snow.

"We *are* escaping!" Santa said. "Do you want to come and try driving this thing? No? Didn't think so."

Finklefoot jumped onto Belsnickel's back and kicked him in the side.

"Ow, you little fucker!" Belsnickel pushed back onto his haunches

"Sorry," Finklefoot said. "Completely forgot. If you could chase after the raving lunatic, that would be great." The gun in his hand was still seeping purple smoke; he hoped to god he hadn't broken it.

Belsnickel roared and charged after Krampus, who was making good his escape via the back-alleys of the village. Imagine, if you can, the Reeves/Swayze chase of *Point Break*, but with two giant bearded immortals, one of which carried a squealing elf wearing a pointy hat and a pair of matching dungarees. With me? Okay...

"He's a bit nippy for a big lad," Finklefoot said as Belsnickel leapt over a small fence. It was all the elf could do to stay on the Companion's back.

"I told you," Belsnickel breathlessly said. "He's the strongest out of all of us. That's why everyone knows who *he* is, and why we're just a mention on *his* Wikipedia page."

Finklefoot shook his head. "You'll get your *own* Wikipedia pages after this," he said, clinging on for dear life.

"And the *song*," Belsnickel said. He was catching up to the fleeing lunatic; if only he'd put more thought into what he might do when he reached him. "Don't forget about the song you promised us."

"We'll get a song," Finklefoot said. *Whether it'll be any good*, he thought, *is another matter entirely.*

Krampus, no more than twenty feet in front now, turned and blew into his horn. At some point in the last ten seconds, he'd managed to reload. *Heeeerrrrrrnk!!!* The dart flew from the horn, splitting the air in half. One unlucky snowflake was severed, but that was perhaps a fluke, and Krampus didn't have time to celebrate anyway.

"Look out!" Finklefoot said, but before the final word fell from his lips, Belsnickel jerked back, clutching at his chest as if in the throes of a particularly violent coronary. The dart was in him – boy, was it in him – and in less than a second, the Companion went from fifteen miles an hour to minus three.

Finklefoot jumped clear of the floundering Companion and disappeared beneath the snow, which was, unsurprisingly, colder than a witch's tit.

"Oh, deary me," Belsnickel said, staggering back and forth like a drunken ogre. "Oh, deary, deary me."

"Are you okay?" Finklefoot said, popping up from the snow like some ridiculous version of whack-a-mole.

Belsnickel grunted. "I've been better." He pulled the dart from his chest and examined it with sleepy eyes and blurred vision. The dart dripped with blood – *his* blood – and something gelatinous, like sap from an infected tree. "I'm okay," he said. "Just need to walk it off." He took a step forward, which was a good place to start if one intended to walk something off. Unfortunately, that was where his journey ended and he wilted listlessly into the snow.

Scratching his head, Finklefoot sighed. So much for strength in numbers, and so much for 'size matters'. The only thing the big guys had managed to prove thus far was that it was much harder to dodge poisonous darts if you were built like a brick shithouse.

"Such a shame," a voice said, snapping Finklefoot from his reverie. "We used to be close friends. Not too close, mind. He had awful breath." Krampus crunched through the snow toward the half-submerged elf. He had a look about him; a look that said 'you can clobber me with a bleeding saucepan all you like, but an elephant never forgets'. "Well, I guess this is *it*," he said, pulling a dart from his shroud and dropping it into the horn. "The end. The big finale. The last stand."

"The endgame?" Finklefoot said, training the Anti-Companion Water-Pistol™ on Krampus's head, where it was most likely to inflict the utmost damage. "*Overture?*"

"No, an overture would be at the beginning," Krampus said. "As would a preamble, a prelude, and a foreword."

"That's very *interesting*," Finklefoot said, standing up straight and dusting the snow from his dungarees. "How's about you give yourself up? Put the horn down and put your hands in the air?"

Krampus laughed. "That's not going to work for me," he said. "And nobody likes a sensible ending. I guess we're just going to have to duel, like they did in the old days."

Of course, back in the old days they hadn't used dart-blowing horns or magical water-pistols, but apart from that the analogy was spot-on.

"A duel it is," Finklefoot said. His heart was racing. He'd never been in a duel before. He'd read about them in history books, and from what he remembered, things wouldn't work out too well for one of them. Then there was always that small chance that both would be wounded or killed, like in the infamous duel between Andrew Jackson (US President) and Charles Dickinson (attorney and famous duellist). It might, therefore, go the other way, and neither of them would be harmed, like in the not-so-famous duel between Stevie Wonder (musician) and Stephen Hawking (automaton).

The trick, Finklefoot thought, *is not getting shot.* Nothing more, nothing less…

"So how do we go about this duelling malarkey?" Finklefoot said, if nothing else buying himself another few seconds of life. "Do we stand back-to-back, count to three, walk ten paces, turn and shoot?"

Krampus shrugged. "Not sure I can be bothered with all that," he said. "Maybe we could do it like they did in those spaghetti westerns. We growl at each other for a few minutes. I smoke a cigar. You perspire irrepressibly. We hover over our weapons for dramatic effect, and then one of us dies."

"Okay, let's do that, but maybe you should give the cigar a miss. Those things will kill you."

"How thoughtful," Krampus said, stuffing the loaded horn into the pocket of his shroud. "The only thing missing is an Ennio Morricone score. You know? To build the tension?"

"You want me to hum something?" Finklefoot said as he holstered the Anti-Companion Water-Pistol™. "I could always go whaahw-ahhwahhh…wha..wha..wahhhh."

"No, that's terribly distracting," Krampus said. "Perhaps silence is best."

And so they stood. Two duellists, too tired to obey the rules of a genuine duel. Krampus, the creator of The Human Santapede (with or without brackets) and Finklefoot, The Fat Bastard's second-in-command (one of them, anyway). Standing in the snow as more snow fell all around. Neither backing down, but at least one of them praying for a bolt of fortuitous lightning to strike the other where he stood.

This is how it ends, Finklefoot thought. Not with a whimper, which would have been far preferable, but with an almighty bang. Finklefoot's trousers squeaked, as was their wont, as he shifted nervously from tiny foot to tiny foot.

If only, he thought, Trixie had clobbered the lunatic harder with the saucepan. But it was too late now for such fruitless wonderings. This was how it was meant to end.

Any minute now…

It was, in fact, seven minutes later when Krampus lunged for his weapon. Finklefoot was half asleep, and so it was, he thought, the miracle of miracles when a liquorice Catherine wheel slapped Krampus across the face.

"What the fu…" was all that Krampus could manage before a giant strawberry lace lashed him hard across the neck. The horn, now in his hand, dropped to the snow as more and more sweetie treats pelted into him, leaving marks and welts and bruises wherever they landed.

Finklefoot fumbled for the water-pistol, but fumblings weren't enough. Not that it mattered. Krampus had fallen to his knees, and was being bombarded with every sweet imaginable by things that had yet to reveal themselves.

"No, please stop!" Krampus whined, just as a sugar-coated lemon-jelly wedge whipped across his cheek.

There was no reprieve, though, as candy after candy walloped into him. As if he knew his days were numbered, he assumed the position (anyone who has taken a kicking knows exactly *what* position) and began to scream. It was an odd sound to come from such a hulking beast, but you know what they say. *The bigger they are, the shriller they squeal*, or something to that effect…

"2nd Unit! Fire!" a voice commanded from the snow to Finklefoot's right. He turned to see

Hattie Hermann sitting astride one of the reindeer (Vixen? Blitzen? Fucked if they didn't all look the same). Beside her, an army of elves were plucking sweets from buckets and launching them toward the fallen Companion. It would have been hilarious had it not been so damned ridiculous.

"Cannon one! On my mark!" Hattie bellowed. She was far too manly to screech. "FIRE!"

A loud explosion rocked the night. Snow fell from rooftops and trees. Poop dropped from reindeer's arseholes. Finklefoot did the first thing that came to mind, which was *duck*.

It was lucky that he *had* ducked, for something whistled past his head, so close that he felt the wind from it. He also caught a faint whiff of spearmint.

The colossal candy cane slammed into Krampus's shoulder spinning him around. It was then that he saw the army of sneaky elves approaching from the rear, or as it was now known, the front…

"GET HIM!" one elf roared.

"BITE HIS FUCKIN' NOSE OFF!" yelled another.

"WILL WE NEED TETANUS SHOTS AFTER!?" a rather sensible elf enquired.

Finklefoot clambered to his feet and watched as Krampus disappeared beneath a tide of flailing elf appendages and pointy hats. Snow and blood flew up into the air as the savage assault went on, and on, and...

"Did we *get* him?" said a booming, and yet lethargic, voice. Finklefoot thought he had seen it all, but the appearance of The Human Santapede, sitting astride five confused-looking reindeer, proved him wrong.

"We *did!*" Hattie Hermann said, a little too smugly for Finklefoot's liking. "He's under that pile of elves, there."

Finklefoot finally managed to get the Anti-Companion Water-Pistol™ out of his waistband. For what good it had done, it might as well have been, like its Fat Bastard owner, firing blanks.

"Ah, Finglefleet!" Santa said, smiling down at Finklefoot. The reindeer he was bleeding all over didn't look half as happy. "Excellent work! I understand this wouldn't have been possible without your assistance."

"Hthrthertherth!" Mrs Claus said.

"Will you pipe *down!*" Santa said. "Nobody cares what you have to say. And yes, I know what you've been up to with my workforce, and I therefore have no choice but to demote you to third-in-command. Should be ashamed of yourself. Oh, and this one's on the house..." And with that, The Fat Bastard went very red very quickly as he pushed something terrible from his body.

Jessica Claus gagged. Jessica Claus passed out.

"Sorry about that," Santa said to Finklefoot. "Now, let's discuss your reward. I remember you said something about a song? Oh, and if you know of a good surgeon, that would be most useful in the coming hours. So, this song? Does it *have* to be by Elton John? He's a tough man to get hold of, and I've got this friend who owes me a favour or two. He's had quite a lot of success with Christmas songs. I think you're going to…"

The (In)Human Santapede (Finklefoot - A Christmas Saviour)

Lyrics and Music by Noddy Holder

Introduction
Iiiiiiiiiiiiiiiittttttsssss
Chrissssssssssssssstmaaaaaaaaaasssssss!!!!

Verse One
When his snowblower disappeared from Santa's Hall,
Krampus did set out to disgust and appal,
Does he stitch them arse to face,
'Cos his surgeon skills are ace?
Does he sever all their tendons just in case?

Adam Millard

Chorus
So here it is, Merry Christmas,
Everybody's arse to face,
Shitting down each other's throats,
A yuletide disgrace.

Verse Two
But now Krampus never counted on Finklefoot,
Or his Companion friends who also like a rut,
Did they save the sutured reindeer?
Did they save Christmas that year?
Or did Krampus shoot them down with his horny spears?

Chorus
So here it is, Merry Christmas,
Everybody's arse to face,
Shitting down each other's throats,
A yuletide disgrace.

Verse Three
The Companions fell but lived to tell the tale,
And Mrs Claus still fucks small folk that are male,
And now Krampus is in prison,
And a hero now has risen,
And the Santapede was chopped up with precision.

Chorus
So here it is, Merry Christmas,

Everybody's arse to face,
Shitting down each other's throats,
A yuletide disgrace.

Verse Four
So Christmas was saved and evil was defeated,
And the elves have since been treated,
Brushed their teeth to get the taste out,
Rudolph's got a brand new snout,
Not as glowy, but it's better than going without.

Repeat Chorus until everyone starts to cry...
Fade out...

Adam Millard

WWW.ADAMMILLARD.CO.UK
WWW.CROWDEDQUARANTINE.CO.UK

THE HUMAN SANTAPEDE

Adam Millard

Lightning Source UK Ltd.
Milton Keynes UK
UKOW05f0358041114

241003UK00002B/3/P